I'D RATHER BE FAMOUS

'A witty and sometimes pungent look at TV fame'
– Guardian

Pete Johnson says, 'My sister Linda helped me to write *I'd Rather Be Famous* by appearing on the TV show *Blind Date*. She was one of the three pickees. To her amazement, she was chosen. She won a day in Bologna with a guy who did impressions of Benny Hill! Linda gave me some brilliant behind-the scenes insights. And she enjoyed herself. Well, I think she did!'

D1434170

Pete Johnson has been a film extra, a film critic for Radio 1, an English teacher and a journalist. However, his dream was always to be a writer. At the age of ten he wrote a fan letter to Dodie Smith, author of *The Hundred and One Dalmatians*, and together they communicated for many years. Dodie Smith was the first person to encourage him to be a writer.

He has written many books for children, as well as plays for the theatre and Radio 4, and is a popular visitor to schools and libraries.

Some other books by Pete Johnson

FAKING IT
THE COOL BOFFIN
MIND READER DOUBLE
THE PROTECTORS
TEN HOURS TO LIVE

For younger readers

BUG BROTHER
PIRATE BROTHER

I'D RATHER BE
FAMOUS

PETE JOHNSON

PUFFIN BOOKS

PUFFIN BOOKS

Published by the Penguin Group
Penguin Books Ltd, 80 Strand, London WC2R ORL, England
Penguin Putnam Inc., 375 Hudson Street, New York, New York 10014, USA
Penguin Books Australia Ltd, 250 Camberwell Road, Camberwell, Victoria 3124, Australia
Penguin Books Canada Ltd, 10 Alcorn Avenue, Toronto, Ontario, Canada M4V 3B2
Penguin Books India (P) Ltd, 11 Community Centre, Panchsheel Park, New Delhi – 110 017, India
Penguin Books (NZ) Ltd, Cnr Rosedale and Airborne Roads, Albany, Auckland, New Zealand
Penguin Books (South Africa) (Pty) Ltd, 24 Sturdee Avenue, Rosebank 2196, South Africa

Penguin Books Ltd, Registered Offices: 80 Strand, London WC2R ORL, England

www.penguin.com

First published in Great Britain by Methuen Children's Books Ltd 1989
Published by Mammoth an imprint of Reed Consumer Books Ltd 1991
Published in Puffin Books 2001
5

Copyright © Pete Johnson, 2001

Set in 11.5/15.5 Linotype Goudy
Typeset by Rowland Phototypesetting Ltd, Bury St Edmunds, Suffolk
Made and printed in England by Clays Ltd, St Ives plc

British Library Cataloguing in Publication Data
A CIP catalogue record for this book is available from the British Library

ISBN 0–141–31546–6

I'd Rather Be Famous

Just over a year ago my careers' teacher did an impression of the Incredible Hulk. I'll never forget it. One moment she was being boring and normal. The next, her eyes suddenly became blank and expressionless exactly like the Hulk's eyes do when it's about to turn all muscly.

I watched my careers' teacher with a new fascination. Was she about to transform herself? Any change would have been welcomed. But disappointingly, all she did was shake her chins at me and ask how old I was.

'You know how old I am,' I said. 'Fifteen.'

'Yes, well – what you've just said makes me think you're no more than five. It really is time you grew up, Jennifer.'

And what had I said to cause all this high-powered anger? Just one sentence, that's all.

She'd asked me what job I wanted to do. And I said – this is exactly what I said – 'I'd like to appear on television as a presenter or host of a chat show.'

Well, you wouldn't think saying that would make her go crazy, would you? Still, her reaction confirmed my belief that all school does is prepare you for a boring life.

After that, I deliberately sabotaged the rest of my careers interview. I admit that. I mean, when she asked me where I lived I said, 'Oh, I live on the wild side.' And when she asked me if I'd like to train for the Services, I said, 'I'd rather be famous.' I just went totally silly. And in the end she ordered me out. It was brilliant.

Still, in a way, she had the last laugh. For, at the end of the fifth year when most of my friends had already left school and were getting on with the next bit of their lives, I was still grounded, going nowhere.

And when my mum went down with me to the careers' office in town, the guy there – a thin, weedy-looking man with a giant Adam's apple – kept shuffling through my papers as if he couldn't believe how bad my GCSE grades were. I was pretty surprised by them myself. I mean, I hadn't worked, so I didn't expect much but even so . . . and no, I'm not going to tell you what they were. You'd only weep.

'Did you enjoy any subjects at all at school?' asked the careers' officer.

I shook my head.

'You must have enjoyed something.' He was getting desperate now. There was something. But it was no use telling him. I'd like to tell you, though.

We were doing these talks in English and I gave a talk on the life of a shoelace. It was really daft – I even talked about a shoelace's mating habits – but the class loved it. I had them in fits of laughter; even the teacher was smiling (if rather reluctantly). And the applause afterwards – no, it wasn't just the applause – it was the way everyone looked at me, as if they really liked me.

Of course, I'd got laughs in class before but this was different: I was in front of an audience, just like a presenter is on television, only my audience wasn't as easy as theirs – the class slow hand-clapped some talks.

I'd found the one job I could do. Sometimes I'd see a TV presenter straining to be jolly and friendly and not even beginning to succeed. And I'd *know* I could do much better than that. For I am a naturally smiley and chatty person. Ask anyone. And I can put people at their ease and look interested in what they're saying, even when I'm not. (Careers' officers excepted.) And I'm bright, lively and friendly – plus I love appearing in front of an audience.

In fact, I have all the qualities needed to be a presenter. And I'm not being big-headed. I know I have very little talent. I can't sing, dance, act – well, you name it – I can't do it. I doubt very much if I can do anything, except be a TV presenter.

Now you know a lot more about me than that careers' officer ever did. For I never told him any of this. I just said, 'I'd like a job that's exciting.'

And straightaway he and my mum started exchanging these smiles as if I was about four and had just said something dead cute.

'Life is rarely as exciting as we'd like,' said the careers' officer, still smiling. 'In fact, most of the time it is really very ordinary and mundane.'

And I thought that was such a SAD, NEGATIVE thing for anyone to say, let alone a careers' officer. And there was my mum nodding in agreement with him.

When we were back home I challenged her. 'I thought you said life was what you made it,' I said. My mum paused in the middle of her eighty-third cigarette that day. 'Life *is* what you make it,' puff, puff, 'provided you don't expect too much.'

'You've never added that last bit before,' I said.

'Well, I'm older and wiser now.'

A week later the careers' officer rang up to say he'd got me an interview at Vaughan's, this large electrical shop. And, shock, horror, I got the job and there was rejoicing in the land, especially as I did well at first. Three and a half weeks later I walked out. No one knows why, not even Mum, although she thinks she does. I mean, it's no big scandal or anything. Don't think that. It's just – well, I'd rather not talk about it just yet – if you don't mind.

Anyway, after that fiasco my mum and I had another long chat about life and the importance of education. My mum is currently out three nights a week at evening classes and is getting really high on the whole joy-of-learning trip. So we decided I'd go back to school and do retakes. I'm still there, just. I float in for about ten minutes a week. The rest of the time I skive. How pathetic. I know.

And now it's the night before New Year's Eve and the spring term is just three days away. And here I am, watching television and just burning up with anger because the girl on there is so stiff and awkward – even her smile's all lopsided. I could be so much better than her!

Usually when I say this Adam's with me and he just grins and says, 'Why do you want to waste your time going on there?' When I asked Adam who he liked best on TV he said the man who works Sooty, and the mad old guy in *Scooby Doo* who always says, 'You pesky kids' when he's unmasked as the villain. Television's just a big joke to Adam.

Hang on, you don't know who Adam is, do you? Sorry, he's my boyfriend (he introduced me to some of his friends recently as 'my lady', which I rather liked). And rather amazingly, we've been going out together for eleven and a half months.

I suppose you could say we're getting serious. Certainly not a day passes when I don't see Adam – until today, that is. He's left to spend the New Year with his mother and sister in Winchester. His parents (like mine) are separated. Only he lives with his dad.

Just before Adam left he put this note through my door headed, 'Things I like and love about Jen'. I'm far too modest to show it to you. Well, I'll just show you the beginning –

> **Things I like and love about Jen**
> Watching her slowly get merry.
> When she lets me play snooker with my mates.
> The way she sits in a pub working out who's with who.
> The way she's never in a bad mood.
> When she takes me out on my birthday . . .

It goes on for two pages like that. A4 pages, too. Then there's a third piece of paper which he's headed, 'Things I dislike about Jen'. And underneath he's written in large capitals: NONE.

I really wish Adam were here now. And yet, I hate myself for wishing that. For I don't want to end up like those girls who just live for boyfriends. And there's more to my life than Adam. Or there should be.

My life – as another year ends I can't help thinking what a waste it's all been so far. If only I could get started on my TV career. Then everything would be transformed. Even the bad bits.

I sit staring into my mirror. I spend hours sitting there, for I see something no one else sees.

I see me on television in very bright colour, like they have in 1950s movies, talking about my life. And it's only then my life seems to make sense and to have any pattern to it. Today I am being interviewed by a smart young guy – we'll call him Trendy.

TRENDY: Now, Jen, your life hasn't been all good, has it? For instance, when you were fifteen your father walked out on you and your mother, is that right?

ME: That's right. And a week before Christmas, too.

TRENDY: Just why exactly did he leave?

ME: His reason was both sordid and unoriginal: he ran off with his secretary.

TRENDY: And do you see him much any more?

ME: No, and I don't care because my mum's there for me. And she's a real fighter. The day after Dad left her – she went out and got her old job back as feature writer on the local paper. The day after!

TRENDY: I think you're something of a fighter yourself, Jen. Before you became a TV star you had a lot of disappointments, didn't you?

ME: A few hundred disappointments, actually. That's all the rejection slips I received. I wrote off applying to be a presenter on every show I could think of. And I varied the style. Some of the letters were deep and serious, others were more larky and amusing, a few were just desperate. But the answers I received were identical – very short, very polite and most definite: Get lost! The rejection letters were so alike I even began to wonder if they didn't have a special computer somewhere that just spewed out rejection letters all day. If so, this meant I was spending all my time corresponding with a computer. No wonder I got depressed.

During one holiday I even travelled up to the television studios. And every day for a week I hovered outside, praying some TV producer would see me and spot my star potential. To help things along I smiled winningly at anyone who looked important and collected some mighty peculiar looks, too. (*Audience laugh.*) In the end I stopped because I knew I was just making myself look silly, degrading myself really . . . (*I falter.*)

TRENDY: But you never gave up, did you? Why?

ME: I don't know, really. I had this feeling that I was destined for something else. And I just couldn't see myself leading an ordinary life. Plus I knew that if someone gave me a chance I'd be good on television. Well, I hoped I'd be good on television, for I certainly wasn't good anywhere else. I really wasn't, you know. (*Audience laugh.*)

TRENDY: Well, Jen, now you're a well-loved TV personality and wherever you go you're recognised and have people begging for your autograph. I suppose it's all a bit of a nuisance now.

ME (*sincerely*): No, not for a moment. I'm grateful to my fans. And if my fans want to stop and talk to me on the street and ask for an autograph, well, that's fine. My fans are really important to me . . .

I turn away from my mirror. If only, if only . . . that day-dream would come true.

'Good evening and a warm welcome to each and every one of you . . .' A new presenter's voice comes out of the television now. He sounds so close and confiding as he chatters away, just a few centimetres away from me. How can he be so near and yet so totally unreachable?

I lie back. Everything seems flat and hopeless. And yet I mustn't give up hope, must I? My dream can still happen. I've got to make it happen. But how? What is there left to do?

Answers on a postcard, please.

New Year's Eve:
Something Earth-shattering

I've two best friends, Liz and Kay, and until quite recently we went round everywhere together. They were both just like an extension of me, somehow.

How things change! Tonight Liz invited me to go with her and her boyfriend Mark to the party at the village hall. She said, just because Adam's away that was no reason for me to stay in on New Year's Eve. And I agreed with her – yet still I hesitated, and for a reason I could never tell Liz.

You see, I think her boyfriend's a toss-pot. I remember the first time I saw Mark. He was sitting in a car reading the *Financial Times* and going, 'I see the FT share index is down twenty points today.' I hate it when teenagers act like 56-year-olds. I really do.

Worse though was when Mark asked me what job Adam did and I said, 'He's a warehouse personage.' Then Mark goes, 'Well, I've never heard it called that before,' and he smirked at me in such a way that I knew he was feeling superior both to Adam and me. Mark, by the way, spends his days poncing around in a bank wearing a blue pin-striped suit and is Very Important.

But I decided that not even Mark could make me stay in when the rest of the universe was out celebrating. So at eight o'clock Mark's black Beetle convertible draws up outside my house and when Mark gets out I nearly crack up. And he's grinning all over his face, saying, 'You're really shocked, aren't you? I can tell.'

For Mark is wearing a black T-shirt and ripped jeans. And he thinks he looks so hip and cool and hard, even though it is obvious to anyone that the rips in his jeans have been put in by the shop: they're designer rips, not natural rips.

But he keeps saying to me, 'You never knew I was like this, did you?' while Liz keeps looking at me, almost willing me to be nice to Mark. And I am nice. (Comes naturally!) But Liz worries me.

I mean, when they come in for tea, Liz rushes out to the kitchen to tell me in hushed tones that Mark is very funny about his tea and he must have only half a teaspoon of sugar and literally just one drop of milk in his cup. And she's so anxious about the whole thing, I can't believe it. For Liz used to be so wild. I tell you if she saw a boy she liked at a party she'd just storm up to him and say, 'Excuse me, but are you wearing boxer shorts?' and then, 'Well, go on, prove it.' And she was so mean to her boyfriends. She used to say, 'Treat 'em mean, keep 'em keen.'

But tonight she spends the whole party staring at Mark. And she seems so prim – I hate using that word about a best friend. But I must be honest and the truth is Liz is now very prim. Is that Mark's fault or the fact that Liz – unlike Kay and me – has a job now? For that can change people, too. I don't know. I just hope Liz doesn't change any more.

The party itself is all right and just before midnight something momentous happens. Clare and Geoff get engaged! They're the first people from my year at school to get engaged. Now, I'm not exactly surprised. I mean, I remember at the fifth-year final assembly when the headmaster suddenly stopped his speech to say, 'I'm sorry, I'm very liberal but I won't have this. I'm sorry.' And he was pointing at Clare and Geoff who – shock, horror – had their arms around each other (they weren't kissing or anything, though). And the headmaster goes, 'You either stop that now or you both leave.' And without a word they both left the room arm in arm and then we all started clapping. I tell you, it was brilliant.

So, no, I'm not surprised they've got engaged. It's just, it represents something and it sets me wondering when I'll get engaged. And I know a lot of other people there are suddenly wondering that, too.

And then it is midnight. Soon everyone's kissing everyone else. And I'm wondering if Adam is kissing anyone now and how good it'd be if he walked in. (All evening I've been asked where he is.) Still, the great thing about New Year's Eve is for about an hour all the people you hate are your friends. I even exchanged wet kisses with Mark.

Just for the record, I also get chatted up several times – all nerds. One guy with buck teeth and no neck, who spends the party leering round corners, suddenly slimes over to me and says, 'Would you hold it against me if I said you had a lovely body?' I gently advise him to get some new chat-up lines.

Shortly after midnight Kay – my other best friend – rushes in fresh from another encounter with the great love of her life: Stevie Lee, the TV star. He's the one with very dark curly hair who's got a front tooth missing which some people think goofy (me) and others very cute (Kay). He's currently starring on TV in an advert for mints and on stage in Stevenage playing Buttons in *Cinderella*. And Kay hasn't missed a performance. But sitting through twenty-seven evenings of 'He's behind you!' has been worth it, for now she exchanges a few seconds of chat with Stevie Lee every night after the show. Tonight he even gave her three tickets for next Thursday.

Kay offers the other tickets to Liz and me. And Liz immediately and rather rudely, I thought, declines, saying she's far too busy. So then I have to say that I'd love to go and I'd bring Adam too. Later Liz says to me, 'I do think Kay should have grown out of these crushes by now. I bet she still has pin-up pictures all over her wall.'

And I think, so what if she has? She's only sixteen and a half. And anyway, I still have photos on my wall, although most of my idols are dead. In fact they all are – James Dean, Marilyn Monroe, Humphrey Bogart, Montgomery Clift. I find it's safer liking stars who are dead. At least they can never disappoint you. You see, once I met this star – who shall remain nameless – that I'd been crazy about. And in the flesh he was so, so ignorant I couldn't believe it and I went right home and tore up all my pictures of him.

But, to return to the party. Just as we are leaving I go over and congratulate Clare again. And she says, 'It's your turn next – yours and Adam's.' I smile and say, 'Oh, I don't know.' But Clare says, 'I've seen you two together. You see if I'm not right.'

I'm thinking about that now. And part of me is very excited. For I would like to get engaged and sometimes I can see Adam and me married, sitting in front of a huge fire locked in a passionate embrace, our dog snoozing beside us.

But then there's another part of me that's wondering, could I marry someone who's just a warehouseman? And I don't mean that to sound snobby. I really don't. It's only, say I marry Adam in a year or two and he's still only a warehouseman (this is likely; Adam has very little ambition) that'll mean I'll have to work too, just so we can save enough to buy a tiny semi on an estate choked up with tiny semis. Next I'll have a baby ... two years later I'll have another one and then ... well, that's it. That's my life – a devoted wife and mother who also does some part-time job like very junior sales assistant or something.

And it isn't enough. I don't want to just fade away down some back street with Adam, and then end up on a gravestone with no one remembering who I am. I want to make my mark, show everyone I'm here and sign at least a few autographs before I die.

And I know, until that happens, there'll always be this great gaping emptiness in my life which no one can fill.

Not even Adam.

Saturday, 2 January:
I Dare Myself to Do Something

I'm watching TV in bed and the usual crew are on, all talking and laughing and showing their fillings. And I think, I could do that. Usually when I think this I can also laugh at myself, the way Adam does. But tonight I can't laugh for I have something stuck in my throat. Envy . . .

And frustration. Why won't someone give me a chance? That's all I need. Just one lucky break. Just one proper answer to my letters. Please!

Finally, I can't listen to all the TV laughter any more. It's just like eavesdropping on a party I'll never be invited to. So I bury my head under the sheets instead. You may wonder why I don't just switch the TV off. Well, you see such a process will involve leaving a very warm bed – a task my body is always most reluctant to perform.

So when I wake up this morning I open my eyes and then promptly close them again. Have I really just seen a grizzled, overweight potato in a chunky sweater? A closer inspection of my television reveals that it isn't exactly a potato, it's a Carly Carter, a sub-human species also known as a TV game show host. You must have seen him. He's the guy whose smiles always drop down past his chin.

Actually, he fascinates me. I think it's the way he manages to contain all that fat in one pair of trousers. I imagine him each morning holding his breath while carefully squeezing in every last particle of flab. For Carly, putting on his trousers must be rather like packing a bulging suitcase.

Carly is the 'special guest' on this early morning phone-in. 'So if you've got a question for Carly,' pipes the announcer – a thin, jerky guy with a laugh that's more like a nervous twitch – 'ring us now on . . .'

What would I ask Carly? When was the last time you saw your feet? Disappointingly, no one asked him that. Instead, all Carly's questions are really just cues for jokes. Quick sample:

CALLER FROM SOUTHAMPTON: 'Carly, will you be joining any new clubs this year?'

CARLY: 'Well, I wanted to join Paranoids Anonymous. I know they hold meetings every Thursday but they won't tell me where.'

Laugh – I nearly did. It's painful but hypnotic. What amazes me though is the way everyone is so pleased, if not thrilled, to be talking to Carly. They greet him as if he is a long-lost relative of theirs or something. One woman even invites him to stay – for free – in her hotel by the sea as she thinks he's been looking 'under the weather' recently. When I hear that, my throat starts feeling all clogged up again. Even a nerd like Carly Carter can touch the power, the special power you gain from appearing on TV. Just put your face on TV and soon you'll have more of a place in people's lives than their next-door neighbours.

At the end of the phone-in the announcer says, 'Now, Carly has an important message for all you teenagers out there about his show, *Who Do You Woo?*, which starts a brand-new series this Friday. Just in case you haven't got *Who Do You Woo?* in your area yet, here's a quick low-down.

'*Who Do You Woo?* is, I suppose, a cross between a talent contest and a dating agency. This boy in a mask comes on stage and tells Uncle Carly he's looking for a date. Then the boy sits behind a desk while three girls, also in masks, take it in turns to tell him why he should invite them to join him on his fantasy date. Sometimes the girls give a little talk, usually they sing or tell jokes. And at the end of all this the boy makes his choice and then comes the great unmasking.

'In the second half a girl makes her choice between three boys. The following week, we see edited highlights of the two couples' fantasy dates. It may sound corny but this show's catching on here really fast.'

And then I have a brainstorm. Carly Carter suddenly leans forward, beams and says, 'Friends, we're looking for teenagers to appear on our new series of *Who Do You Woo*? So, if you're between sixteen and twenty-one, unattached but with a good sense of fun, then why not write and tell us about yourself. Just a few lines. Then we'll send you an application form. The address is . . .' And, to my amazement, I copy the address down.

Of course, I'm not seriously thinking of applying. Adam would go mad for a start. And the show itself – well, it's distinctly tacky and not at all what I'd had in mind for my TV debut. But still, they are looking for people, in fact, practically begging them to apply. And doesn't it seem strange to you that, for the first time ever, I should leave my TV on all night and then wake up just in time to hear about *Who Do You Woo*? It's as if, well, I don't want to be too mysterious about this, but it's as if I was meant to hear that announcement, destined to hear it, in fact.

You're laughing. Well, don't, because I've written the letter already. Take a look?

Dear Carly Carter,

I was very interested to hear you are looking for applicants for Who Do You Woo? – well, look no further.

My name is Jennifer. I am sixteen and a half, small-ish, slimmish, with blonde curly hair and I am always smiling. My main hobby is watching dead stars of the 1950s. Other hobbies – well, how about scuba diving, shark fishing, donkey trekking, freefall parachuting and brain surgery on Friday afternoons?

As you see, I also have a very active imagination. To conclude, in my slightly biased opinion I will be a real asset to your great (creep, creep) show. So why not put me to the test?

Yours, hoping to hear soon.

What do you think? Yes, I know I sound about eight from that letter. The trouble is, in my first attempts I sounded about eighty-eight. ('With reference to your announcement . . .') It's quite a hard letter to write really, especially as I despise the show. So shall I send the above off?

Adam will go crazy, of course. I shiver. So, dare I?

Yes. I DARE! And I'm going to post it off right now – before I lose courage.

Sunday, 3 January:
Meet the Latest Old Married Couple

'How many Goths does it take to change a light bulb? None. They prefer to sit in the dark.' Only one person tells me silly jokes like that.

I meet Adam's train at 7.00 this evening. The first moment I see him I feel strangely shy. Is this really the person who knows me better than anyone else? Then he waves and grins and my heart does its usual aerobics.

He's wearing his thick, zip-up sweater, tight jeans – even though his legs are really too thin for them – and the shoes I bought for his birthday which he hated on sight, but still faithfully wears.

I ask him about his holiday with his mum, sister and prospective step-dad. He talks about his mum and how great she is.

'I'd love to meet her. When's she coming down here?'

'Don't know,' says Adam. 'She's really happy now. It's good to see her so happy . . .' He changes the subject. 'Been to any wild parties, then.'

'Hundreds.'

'Suppose you're quite disappointed I'm back.'

'Incredibly disappointed.'

Actually, I'm so pleased to see Adam I'm embarrassing myself. And yet, the weird thing is, Adam and I went to the same school – he's a year older than me – and I knew him very vaguely for years without being the slightest bit interested in him.

Then, quite out of the blue, he rang me. That was when I was in the fourth year (right at the end) and he'd just left school. And unfortunately, Dad answered the phone and instead of leaving me alone to talk to Adam as any normal father would do, he hovered behind me doing his impression of a coffee percolator right down my ear. So Adam and I had this incredibly stilted conversation, not helped by the fact I wasn't sure for ages exactly who he was. (I knew a few Adams.) Anyway, I turned him down (ahh) but more out of embarrassment than anything else.

Afterwards Dad said smugly, 'You can't be too careful with callers like that, you know.'

Then – and how about this for hypocrisy? – two weeks

after ruining my love life my dad leaves home in hot pursuit of his own.

Anyway, for months afterwards Adam totally ignored me. I didn't blame him at all. Once or twice I was even tempted to go up and just say hello to him or something but I was scared he might say something very nasty to me. (I'm quite brave except where there's a chance I might be rejected. Then I'm a total coward.)

I was at a party almost a year ago now when Adam walked in. And he looked so awful I was quite glad I hadn't gone out with him. But, to my great surprise, he came over to me. I think he was quite drunk but we spoke very politely until he rather stunned me by asking, 'Do you remember when I rang you up and asked you out?' And we both laughed a little too loudly until he said, 'I was wrecked when you turned me down last time. So you won't turn me down again, will you?'

And I thought, well, if he wants to go out with me that much he's obviously got good taste if nothing else. So I agreed, never expecting him to last longer than any of my other boyfriends (a month at the most).

Yet, almost a year later, Adam and I are still together – and in danger of turning into an old married couple. Don't ask me why. To be honest, if I saw Adam's picture in a magazine or something I wouldn't fancy him. He's got dark brown hair for a start, which I don't normally like (I prefer jet black or blond). I suppose he is fairly muscular, well, he's got quite thick arms, but otherwise he's of average height and weight and with slightly above the average number of zits. There are lots of people like Adam walking around. You'll know at least six.

Only Adam *is* different from all the others. Perhaps it's his eyes – denim blue. Yes, that must be part of it. For you only have to look into Adam's face to find yourself telling him everything. Lots of girls say that. Even Liz, who wasn't wild about him at first, says he's very sympathetic. Mind you, when I told Adam this he smiled and said the fact that girls like talking to him shows they don't fancy him.

I said, 'That's rubbish.'

But he explained. 'Girls can't talk to the boys they really like. And I've always been the type of person girls can talk to.'

When I told Mum this she said, 'Adam's the sort of boy who, when he's twenty, will have queues of girls after him.' My mum's always really nice to Adam. I mean, really nice. She trusts him and so do I.

Incidentally, Adam and I haven't gone the full distance yet.

I hate that phrase but then all the words for sex are pathetic. I mean, 'having it off' really sets the heart singing, doesn't it? As for 'bonk' – well, that might just about describe what sheep do to each other but nothing else. I don't even like 'making love', because it sounds phoney. I could imagine Mark writing in his filofax: making love 8.00 p.m. to 8.05 p.m. sharp. I think someone – a girl – should invent a new phrase.

Still, whatever the phrase, Adam and I haven't. We've come pretty close – right on the brink, you might say. And I like being on the brink, especially of something I think will be sensational. Only, I'd hate it not to be sensational or for Adam to be disappointed or me, for that matter. And you never know, do you?

But tonight we're sitting in this restaurant where they're having a party for four-year-olds who scream a lot (all the four-year-olds were given balloons and Adam insisted on asking for a balloon for me. He kept his face completely straight while he was doing it too), when he says, 'How about if you and I go to the seaside this Easter? We could go to Brighton.' I nod enthusiastically and then he goes on, 'I'll book us a room, then.'

A room. I think he said 'a room', but I'm not sure and I can't ask him because – well, you can't, not straight out like that. It sounds so prim. And anyway, why shouldn't we share a room? We're old enough. We love each other. So why not?

No. I hope Adam did mean one room and it will be wonderful. Probably.

Monday, 4 January:
New Term

The day begins terribly. By some freak of nature I arrive at school on time, so I'm immediately hustled into first-day-of-term assembly (very like end-of-term assembly only longer and much much sadder). The whole school has to remain standing except for the sixth form. We're allowed to sit on benches in the front. Back in September we filled two benches. Now there are just eighteen and a quarter of us (I'm there so rarely I only count as a quarter) and we all huddle pathetically together – Kay and I whispering gossip. Then this teacher starts reading out notice after notice, her face pink with excitement. She's obviously having a great time. In fact, reading aloud a notice about what entrance to use after lunch is probably better than going out on a Saturday night for her.

After assembly, another teacher enjoys herself by checking everyone's hands and wrists for jewellery. On no account must anyone try and decorate their grey school uniform or stamp their individuality upon themselves in any way. So no bangles, no rings, no bright colours, no life.

And I'm just standing in the corridor, reeling slightly from the first-day-of-term heavy polish smell and wondering yet again why every wall in the school has to be the colour of urine, when I'm ambushed by Mucus. Mucus (Miss Murcus to her friends) is my sixth-form tutor, a small tired-looking woman who begins her Geography lesson by standing in front of a map of the world with her hand on her breast and declaring, 'All right. Come on. I didn't volunteer for this, you know.'

I'm summoned to her office, which even on the first day of term is full of decaying coffee cups and folders that look as if they're about to flake away. She has a grave look on her face. I'm to be tried for many sins. And I know instantly what my most evil deed is.

'Jennifer, come on now, just come on. You wouldn't wear such big ones in an office, would you?'

Mucus is pointing at my earrings. As sixth-formers we no longer have to wear uniform but we are supposed to dress in the style appropriate to a dingy office.

'Yes, I would,' I reply firmly. 'And anyway, if offices are

so strict and old-fashioned, why not let us experiment a bit now? Give us at least a taste of freedom.' Then I beam at her. I've found that if ever you answer back to a teacher, always end by smiling in a really friendly way. That really confuses them.

'I woke with a headache this morning,' says Mucus. 'It's gone off now. I do hope it's not going to come back.'

She sniffs loudly. I can't help but feel a tiny stab of sympathy for her. I bet she dreads the beginning of term even more than me. All her classes give her hell.

I let Mucus work through her stock phrases and lay a bet with myself on just when she'll say, 'I can't get inside your head and do the exams for you.' Then, after lecturing me on my lack of work in English, in Maths, in everything, Mucus suddenly asks, 'How's the acting going?' Funny how even the worst teachers can make these lightning changes into a human being.

'Well, it's not so much acting as presenting on TV I want, although I'm interested in acting, too.'

'Get on TV and you'll be a tax exile,' says Mucus. 'They're all tax exiles, aren't they?' She speaks dreamily as if that's what she'd like to be. 'I've some friends who teach acting skills – might be of use to you.'

She burrows about in her office until finally triumphantly drawing out a card headed: 'Acquire Acting Skill today – Let Adrianne and Phyllis Guide You.' The names don't exactly inspire confidence. Nor does the fact they're friends of Mucus. Still, according to the card, Adrianne and Phyllis turned down Equity membership just to teach the young and spot talent. Could they be the ones to find the star quality in me? It's possible, isn't it? Also, if *Who Do You Woo?* comes off (big 'if') these lessons might prove very helpful.

Lessons are every Saturday morning. 'Ten o'clock sharp,' says Mucus. 'I could ring them if you'd like to go.'

'Yes, all right, I'll go. Thank you very much.' Mucus leans back, half smiling. I don't think she gets thanked very often.

'And, Jenny, at least think about what I've said, will you?' she asks, staring at my earrings.

Over lunch – the usual congealed monkey brains – Kay and I talk about Stevie Lee. Last night he exchanged seven sentences with her – a record so far. She asks about Thursday. I say it's fine, even though I haven't asked Adam yet.

By mid-afternoon it's already getting dark and the lights have to go on in all the classrooms. I remember at my first school when the lights went on in the afternoon, that meant it was almost home-time. Yet now, is it really only the afternoon break? Today already feels like two weeks. And can I face another hour of maths? I fear not.

I arrive in the town centre just as this truck is hauling Father Christmas and his sleigh off the top of Woolworths. A cup of coffee is needed to restore me after that distressing sight. I'm served by a girl I know vaguely from my school. She's wearing a cardboard hat and a badge saying, 'Hi, I'm Sue.'

'Still working at Vaughan's, then?' she asks conversationally.

'No, I walked out.'

'Oh no, really? Why?'

'It just didn't work out, you know.'

Sue clearly doesn't, for she returns, fishing, 'I can't believe you left Vaughan's. I thought you'd get on really well there. You're just the type.'

Just as I'm leaving, Sue offers to get me a job at the café. I say thanks all the same but I'm allergic to plastic seats. She laughs, says I haven't changed and tells me to enjoy the rest of my day.

Straight after that conversation I find myself walking towards Vaughan's, returning to the scene of the crime, you might say. I stand peering through the glass just as a woman enters the shop and all the assistants get ready to swoop. I can sense their excitement. Who's going to take her? Gary gets to her first. He often did. I remember him when I worked there – very smooth, very sharp. Ryan, that's the manager, liked him. He liked me, too.

Number One rule is: make the customer feel noticed right away, Ryan said. First thing every morning he'd give us advice and little pep talks, the kind you imagine football managers giving their teams on Saturday afternoons. Only, every day was Saturday afternoon for us.

I watch Gary move closer to the woman. Always go right into your customer's body space, Ryan said. And Gary's making immediate eye contact while he gives her four reasons why she needs a video. Establish needs, then meet them. Then I watch Gary demonstrate the video. Immediately after the demonstration he'll ask her how she wants to pay for it. Be positive, always be positive.

'Can't stay away, can you?' I wheel round. Ryan is staring up at me. He looks like a dissolute leprechaun, being very small, with hooded eyes that can light up or darken very quickly. Immediately he enters my body space, oozing assurance.

'Come to ask for your old job back?' he asks, then before I can reply he says, 'I'll buy you a coffee.'

I feel awkward and embarrassed. I should say, 'No thanks,' and walk away. But instead I follow him back to the café I left only ten minutes earlier. Of course, Sue's eyes are hanging out. I start to recover myself. Ryan's not at all good-looking but he's got an easy confidence that's really quite powerful.

'Two of your best coffees,' he says to Sue, 'and two slices

of cholesterol. I mean cake.' Then to me, 'So what's new?'

I manage a few light-hearted remarks, he leans back smiling. Then in the same easy tone he says, 'I was very upset when you walked out on me, you know.'

'Were you?' Somehow I can't imagine Ryan upset. Angry, mad, revengeful, yes, but upset, no.

'I was very upset. Not every day I lose one of my most promising staff.' He smiles. 'But at least I know why.'

I stiffen.

'You silly girl,' he says.

Now, I'd better just tell you why I left Vaughan's. I should have told you before. It's just a bit shaming, that's all.

You see, when I joined Vaughan's it was *very* competitive. Ryan encouraged that. If you did well and got lots of sales he gave you commission, praised you, treated you like a hero. But at the end of the week if your sales hadn't been so hot – well, the person with the lowest sales had their photograph stuck underneath this poster headed: 'Death of a Salesman'. And if your face appeared underneath that poster three times in a month, you were out. Sacked.

The first two weeks I was there, Rachel made the poster both times. So every time Rachel went into the staffroom she had to pass this humiliating poster of herself – and it was a huge poster, absolutely huge, with black edges all round it as if she'd just died. I tell you that poster gave me the creeps and every time I saw it I said a little prayer that I'd never end up on there.

Still, I was doing really well until my third week – that was when I seemed to bag all the dud customers, the ones who talked a lot but didn't buy anything. By Friday morning I was in trouble. I knew the next face under 'Death of a Salesman' would be mine. I'd be publicly branded a failure and I couldn't handle that. Perhaps it was just too close to the truth – you know, Jennifer screws up *yet again*.

Then Rachel made this sale of some new kitchen equipment. Well, she didn't really make the sale. The customers knew exactly what they wanted. She was just very lucky. But as she was working out the credit agreement she was sent to lunch. I finished the sale and then I put the sale through on to my sales number, not Rachel's. Shocked? So was I.

That bit of cheating meant I beat Rachel, who for the third week running was on the 'Death of a Salesman' poster. I'd like to say I forgot that if Rachel was on the poster three times in a row she'd be out. I'd like to say that. But Rachel never queried how she'd ended up a loser again. She said she'd been expecting it and didn't think she was cut out for the job anyhow. She left that afternoon.

I didn't sleep at all that night. The following day I

phoned Rachel and told her what I'd done – then I resigned. I had to. I hated what the job was doing to me and the way it was showing me sides of my personality I didn't want to see. In my defence, all I can say is I was so scared that Friday, I didn't really know what I was doing. But then that's what people always say after doing something nasty, don't they? I didn't know what I was doing. And it's usually only partly true.

Confession over. Back to Ryan. He's disbelieving, even contemptuous over why I resigned.

He says, 'Actually, you did . . . what's her name . . .?'

'Rachel.'

'You did Rachel a favour. She couldn't sell. She wasn't confident enough, didn't have what it takes. You did, though. You proved it that day. Of course I knew what you'd done to Rachel and I was proud of you.'

'Proud?'

'Yes, for it proved you've got that streak of ruthlessness – and all good sales people have that.'

'No, I haven't. I'm not ruthless,' I cry.

He smiles. 'All right, have it your own way. But if you weren't any good I wouldn't be wasting my time now. I think you've got a future in sales, Jennifer. Customers like you – and, most importantly, they trust you.'

'But really, I'm just conning them into buying things they don't really want, aren't I?'

Ryan's easy manner vanishes, leaving only impatience. 'Anyone who walks into that shop is fair game. Now come on, stop messing. You want your old job back?'

I hesitate.

'What else are you going to do?' he demands.

'Work on TV,' I say rashly.

'TV, that's the biggest con of all,' says Ryan.

He looks at me expectantly. I still hesitate. Despite everything I am very tempted. Then Ryan stands up.

'Come and see me when you're ready to join the real world.' He leaves me to pay the bill.

I arrive home to find a card from Adam. On the front it says, 'I only think of you once a day' and inside it says, 'All Day'.

Thursday, 7 January:
Inflatable Sausages and Stevie Lee

On the night of the Stevie Lee pantomime Adam's down to play in a snooker match.

'But you can play snooker any time,' I say.

'This is a pretty big match, though,' he replies and starts to explain.

I interrupt. 'If you'd rather play snooker with your friends than go out with me, that's fine. No problem at all.'

'Kay will be there with you.'

'Yeah, sure, don't worry about it. You go off and play snooker. Don't bother about me.'

I've always despised girls who use dialogue like that. And now I'm uttering the same mean blackmailing phrases and probably for the same reason – I need to know I come first with someone.

'No one has ever put me first,' I add in a bid for sympathy. It's true though. My dad certainly never has. As for my mum, well, she cares, of course. I mean, I'm up there with the environment and preschool nurseries as one of her main causes. But it's not quite enough, somehow.

Anyway, Adam and I don't talk for a while. I turn the television up while he sits staring into space. He really loves snooker. This is quite a test. Then finally he gets up to go and says, 'What time's this stupid play on Thursday?'

And straightaway I say it doesn't really matter, you go to snooker. But even as I say it I know he'll come to the theatre with me – no question now.

And, sure enough, on Thursday he calls for me promptly at seven. We walk to the theatre where Kay is waiting impatiently for us. She is all dressed up. Only, she's put on too much make-up, the way people do when they're going on stage. In a way, I think Kay sees herself as part of the show now. And the panto itself is a real shock. I mean, I'd no idea pantos were so dirty. The first act has this old dame bending over and calling out to a leering bloke in green, 'Where's my pussy? Can anyone see my pussy?' The second act is mainly about inflatable sausages. And Stevie Lee.

There's so much applause the first time he comes on he has to walk off and start the scene again. He stands there, tucking his chin into his chest and swallowing hard

37

like he has this really bad indigestion before croaking into song. Adam compares his singing to, I quote, 'a goose farting in the fog'. But I think he's just being kind.

Afterwards Kay rushes us round to the stage door. She seems to know most of the girls who are waiting there. One girl, obviously thinking I'm a fan, starts showing me her album of signed pictures, while Adam makes silly faces and tries to make me laugh.

As soon as Stevie Lee appears there's one almighty scrum. A grim-faced Stevie Lee, smaller and spottier than I'd expected, pushes his way through the crowd, avoiding eye contact with everyone until he reaches his car. Then he seems to relax a bit and smiles back at all the pictures of himself waving in the air. When he sees Kay he goes, 'My sandwich girl,' (Kay runs errands for him, that's how she got the free tickets), 'I knew you'd be here tonight.'

'These are my friends Jenny and Adam,' calls Kay.

He tilts his head about forty-five degrees in our direction before charging into his waiting car.

The saddest sight is after he's gone and all the girls start hugging and comforting each other.

'This is sick,' Adam whispers to me.

But I can see that Kay is really upset so I send Adam home and go back with Kay. She takes me on a guided tour of her bedroom walls, which are covered with glossy photographs bearing really affectionate messages, like, 'To Kay. Much love always.' In the middle of the room is a whole collection of loopy scrawls, courtesy of Stevie Lee. I ask Kay why she likes him so much. And she says, 'So many boys are crude and rough but he's different. He's gentle and clean – oh, there's something about him.'

As I'm leaving she says, 'You know, if tonight he'd asked me to jump in his car and go away with him – I would have – without a second's thought.'

And that brings a real lump to my throat. As I know there's no chance of Stevie Lee ever doing that.

Stevie Lee – I don't like him much – but I can't help envying him all his fans. If – no, when – I become famous I'll treat my fans with far more respect than he does. I won't just rush away. No, I'll greet each one personally and talk to them, giving them a special moment to remember always.

Friday, 8 January:
The First Step to . . .

I wake up late, long after Mum leaves for work, and there waiting on the mat for me is the form for *Who Do You Woo?* It goes on for three sides, longer than most job applications. And it's arrived on the same day as *Who Do You Woo?* starts a new series. Is this a good omen? I'm quite into omens, good or bad. But probably this form, too, is sent out by a computer. And there will be hundreds, if not thousands of these forms landing on mats across the country today. Still, I've never received even a form back before. So this could be my first step to . . . I don't quite know, which makes it more exciting.

At half-six, just before *Who Do You Woo?* starts, I go upstairs to my bedroom. Mum's bustling about downstairs and it's hard to concentrate when she's being busy all round you. She's worse when you're watching a corny film. Then she'll sit there laughing and calling out comments like, 'You'll learn kid.' And with Adam not calling round to go to the pictures until half-seven – he's got yet another driving lesson – I settle myself down to study *Who Do You Woo?*, the application form beside me.

And as soon as the programme's jangly, very catchy theme tune starts up, my heart is already beating an extra beat. Then Carly Carter belly-flops into view. He says, 'This is your show, teenagers,' and then spends five minutes telling silly stories about himself. Finally he rubs his hands together, releases one of his matey smiles and says, 'Now let's meet our masked man.'

This guy in a black mask and a black cape swaggers on. Then down the steps comes the first of the masked girls. She has one minute to persuade him to pick her and she spends her minute singing 'Hey, Big Spender', only she doesn't pronounce her S's very clearly so it comes out more like 'Hey, Big Bender'. The second girl does a tap dance which involves a lot of jumping about and twisting. She also gets a big round of applause when she pretends to be playing the guitar. The last girl gives this nudge-nudge talk about how she can do everything a hot-water bottle does and more. He picks her.

The best moment of the show is always the unmasking. First Carly removes the mask, of the two girls who have been turned down but the big moment is when the guy and his date unmask each other. Then the screen turns all misty and the audience go 'Aaah', as the guy and his human hot-water bottle walk off hand in hand to the accompaniment of slurpy music. It'd be dead romantic if only you didn't know he was wishing he'd picked the girl who sang 'Hey, Big Spender'.

Actually, I'd rather not be picked at all than turn out a disappointment. I mean, could you handle someone unmasking you and then gaping at you as if you're a relative of Godzilla? I couldn't. No, if they select me for the show I hope to be in part two. That's when the girls picks her date from three masked boys. I'd enjoy that. Only today, Adam arrives early and ruins everything.

'What are you watching that coffin dodger for?' he says, pointing at Carly Carter.

It's funny, but already I feel a little protective towards the programme – even of Carly Carter.

'It's not such a bad programme,' I say. 'I quite enjoy it.'

'Since when?'

'Oh, I've always enjoyed it.'

Then, in an attempt to try and involve Adam in the programme, I say that, of the three male contestants now hidden beneath suits of armour, the second guy has the best voice. Big mistake!

For straightaway Adam says, 'Nah, he's got a little girl's voice.'

But he's the one who gets picked and when he removes his mask Adam says, 'And look at those eyes – they go about a mile into his head. I bet he's dead shifty. And he has the personality of a frog.'

'I never said I liked him.'

But Adam keeps on slagging this guy off until it starts to get on my nerves. It scares me, too, for if he gets this heavy just because I like someone's voice, what will he do if I go on the programme? This worries me so much I start getting really snappy and by the time we reach the cinema we're hardly speaking.

Luckily the film we see is so brilliant – and scary – we forget we're in a mood with each other. And on the way home I tell Adam about the one scene I hadn't liked. It was when this couple made love in the kitchen. And there was much grunting and panting while her rear bounced up and down on some unwashed cups in the sink. And it was about as romantic as watching my nan's dog trying to get his leg over a cushion.

So then I say to Adam, 'Didn't you think that scene was a bit gross?' And I add hopefully, 'Unrealistic.'

Straightaway he smiles, puts his arm around me and says, 'Don't worry, in real life it's nothing like that. It's much better, as I hope one day to prove to you.'

And he says it so gently I decide that, whatever happens with *Who Do You Woo?*, I will make certain Adam is never hurt.

Anyway, we part on such good terms that Adam even says he'll come to the Drama Club with me tomorrow.

Saturday, 9 January:
Pass the Marble Egg

At the Drama Club Adam and I are met by these two women, both with long grey hair down to their shoulders and wearing Andy Pandy dungarees and extra-long braces. Their first question – wrapped up in a mile of waffle – is Where's your money? It's two pounds a lesson or, as they called it, a session, and Adam has to pay for both of us. When we've paid up they lead us into a hall which reeks of polish, just like school does at the beginning of term. And there, sitting in a semi-circle, is the rest of the class, mainly girls with names like Faber. The two women sit down with us, 'Just so we're not any bigger than you,' and start handing round this marble egg which each one of us in turn is supposed to describe. As I am the last one to hold it I say, 'I think everyone's said everything.' Then it's breathing exercises.

'No, breathe from your diaphragm,' the twins keep squeaking at me until I say, 'I think I've left my diaphragm at home today.' They are not amused.

Next, we each have to find a space in the middle of the room and start describing ourselves. Before I can begin, Faber, who is wearing disgusting pink legwarmers, pirouettes to the front and cries, 'I am a ship on the quayside, fully loaded, with my engines turning but still tied to the quay.' She looks up to the heavens. 'All it takes is one throw of the rope and I'll be away.'

And may she never return.

I begin the next game. One of the grey-haired women (I haven't a clue which is which) starts prancing about in front of us and whispering, 'Follow, follow me.' Then suddenly she stops and cries, 'You're going to open a door now. Go on, go on.' I start opening this invisible door quite convincingly, I think, until she yells, 'No, the door's not there, it's to your right.' I feel like saying, 'Make up your mind,' but I don't because now she's shrieking, 'When you open the door you see the head of . . . what?' She hovers over me, waiting for my answer. And of course, my mind goes totally blank, she's got me so flustered. She repeats her line, even louder this time, 'You see the head of . . .'

'A match,' I say. Please don't ask me why I say that. Anyway, my answer isn't well received and I'm almost shoved out of the way. Adam, who is next, does better; he sees the head of a snake. Faber, of course, sees not one head but thousands.

Afterwards the grey-haired twins cluster round Adam, saying how pleased they are to have such a promising young man in the group. They go on and on. I wouldn't have been surprised if they'd kissed his feet. I really wouldn't. Faber's there too, doing spins and going up on tip-toe around Adam. (Wouldn't you know she also does dancing here on Saturday afternoons.) Until finally, as a kind of afterthought, the aged twins turn on me. 'Of course, we need our backroom people, too. They're very important. Where would we be without someone to organise the refreshments, for instance?'

So that's the talent they've spotted in me – tea-lady. Adam and I have a laugh about it afterwards. But I can't deny how disappointed I am, too. But then I think, what do those grey-haired crows know? They're out of the ark and they're friends of Mucus. Besides, their games have nothing to do with proper acting, have they? I mean, you can't tell me the cast of *EastEnders* spend their rehearsal time passing round marble eggs to each other and pretending to be ping-pong balls or shoelaces.

Tea-lady! I pick up my *Who Do You Woo?* form. I'll show them!

Sunday, 10 January:
A Jade Is Born

What do you most dislike in a man?
Meanness, moles – especially on his back, bad breath, smelly feet.

Briefly describe your most embarrassing moment.
It was at King's Cross Station, when I had my purse snatched. Not only did I never notice but when my purse burst open on the thief, spilling my money everywhere, guess who helped him pick it all up? At the time I felt really pleased with myself for being so kind, even though I did think it a bit strange that the guy I was helping was so anxious to get away from me. Afterwards in the police station when I realised what I'd done, I just wanted to dissolve into the foul tea they kept offering me.

*

Two samples from my *Who Do You Woo?* form which I've just finished. It's taken all afternoon.

They also ask for a recent photo, which must be full length. To check you haven't got a body like a Sumo wrestler, I suppose.

I want to send a snapshot of me looking glamorous in an exotic setting. But in the end the only halfway decent picture I can find is of me outside Stevenage Leisure Centre. Adam, who took the picture, says I look like a model. I think I'm just lucky it's slightly out of focus.

On the back of the photo I add my vital statistics. And now I sign it, not Jennifer but Jade, the name I should have been called. I write it out a few times. Actually, it feels like mine. I take one last peek at my form, at my glittering new name. Go on, Jade – bring me luck. You imagine things happening to someone called Jade, don't you? Then I realise I've spent longer filling in this form than I ever have over homework.

The idea of appearing on *Who Do You Woo?* won't leave my mind. I can actually feel it in my head, sprouting faster and faster, sucking up all my other thoughts. I just can't stop thinking about it. I just can't stop hoping.

Compulsive gamblers are like that, aren't they? Even if they lose all their money – and most of them do – they're still convinced their luck's about to change. Just one more go and they'll hit the jackpot. So then they start selling all their possessions. Whatever happens they won't give up.

And neither will I.

Tuesday, 12 January:
Dad's Three Bombshells

I've just had an awful time with my dad. I've got to think about this. I go into my bedroom. I sit in front of my mirror and see . . .

The programme title *Heart To Heart* flashes up on the screen, and low, rather subdued, flute music can be heard. A guy we shall call Mr Sincerity smiles into view.

MR SINCERITY: Hello and a very warm welcome to *Heart To Heart*, the show in which celebrities open their heart to you. (*Audience clap.*) Tonight, friends, we have just one guest and a much-loved one. But I'm afraid she's not her usual cheerful self today as she's had a bit of a shock. So I know you'll be especially kind to the lovely Jenny, known to her millions of fans as Jade.

(*I enter to the usual huge but respectful applause.*)

MR SINCERITY: Jade, lovely warm applause for you and thoroughly deserved, but I hear you're a little down-hearted today.

JADE: Oh no, it's nothing really. It's just my parents split up – oh, nearly two years ago now. Anyway, today my father invites me out for dinner – for the first time in ages, I might add. Over the lamb chop comes his first poison pellet. He's asked Yvonne to marry him.

MR SINCERITY: Now, just so that our viewers know, Yvonne is the secretary your father ran away with.

JADE: That's right. Then over the chocolate mousse I receive newsflash number two. Yvonne is heavy with child, or will be soon. Actually, she's pretty heavy without child.

MR SINCERITY (*smiling*): And this news shocks you?

JADE: Yes, don't ask me why. He's been bonking her for five years. (*Laughs and gasps from the audience.*)

MR SINCERITY: When your father told you about Yvonne being pregnant, what did you say?

JADE: I said I hope it's a human. (*More laughter.*) No, sorry. Do I sound bitter?

MR SINCERITY: Well, just a little bit, yes.

JADE: It's my father, he's so tacky. Everything he does is tacky. I mean, it's just so typical of him to wait until someone is pregnant before proposing, isn't it?

MR SINCERITY: I'd like to ask . . .

JADE: Hang on. I haven't told you the final bombshell yet.

MR SINCERITY (*smiling*): You mean, there's more?

JADE: Oh yes, there's more. (*Audience laugh.*) My dad also told me over coffee how he's been offered a promotion in Sheffield. And even as he asks me what I think, I know he's already decided. He's going.

MR SINCERITY: Now, let's get this straight, Jade. Today your father told you that soon he'll have a new wife, a new child and a new job. But just where does that leave you?

JADE: Oh, I'll probably see him as often as Adam sees his mum and sister – about twice a year. On my birthday and at Christmas he'll remember he's my dad. I must tell you, though, just as I'm getting out of the car today, my dad goes, 'Yvonne and I thought you'd like your own proper one,' and he hands me my wedding invitation, like he's giving me my first bra or something. He just cracks me up sometimes, he really does.

MR SINCERITY: So at least you haven't lost your sense of humour.

JADE: Oh, you need a sense of humour with my dad.

MR SINCERITY: You and he . . . aren't very close, then?

JADE (*firmly*): No.

MR SINCERITY: How about your mother? Do you get on well with her?

JADE: Everyone gets on with my mum. I mean, if my mum had been alive during the war they'd have streets named after her by now. She'd have been wonderful during the Blitz. I can just see her rushing about, pulling people out of burning buildings, comforting the wounded, organising . . . oh, she'd have done everything. Been a real heroine. Really, she was born out of her time. So she's had to settle with working for a local paper; she edits the arts section and since Dad left she's also written lots of features – mainly controversial ones – and now she's starting a problem page. She's tried to get me writing a few things but it – well, anyway, to get back to my mum. Basically, she's brilliant.

I mean, when Dad walked out on her everyone said, 'How's she going to take it?' and relatives warned me that my mum would be doing a fair bit of weeping and wailing. But it wasn't like that.

Mind you, she swore a lot and then went rather quiet and subdued, just for a week or two. Then I came home one afternoon to find her busy decorating the kitchen. Now she's decorated the whole house and she's joined evening classes in History of Art and Car Maintenance. And if ever she refers to Dad it's always as 'your father', just as if she's handed over all responsibility for him to me, now.

MR SINCERITY: Jade, may I ask you, did *you* cry when your parents broke up?

JADE: What a funny question but, yes, I did. Then I cry easily. I cry at *E.T.*, *Bambi*, *Lassie*, you name it. I cried today, actually, because ... because ... The interview stops there and Mr Sincerity vanishes.

Just why did I cry? Because ... I'll tell you something funny. When I was about five or six, I knew this girl whose father died at the breakfast table. He just suddenly slumped forward into his cornflakes. And for weeks afterwards I was terrified my dad was going to do the same. Sometimes at night I'd even get up and creep into his room to check he was still breathing. I'd stand by the door for ages, watching him or rather watching over him. And here's what's funny – he wasn't that good to me or anything even then. So why did I care so much?

It's just after ten o'clock when I hear Mum come in with a couple of women from her college course. I exchange polite smiles with them and go into the kitchen where Mum's making coffee. I dread telling her about the wedding so much that, in the end, I just blurt it out.

She doesn't say anything for a second or two, just goes on filling the kettle right up to the brim. Then she asks, 'Registry office, isn't it?'

I nod.

'Thought it would be. Very quick in there, like a conveyor belt. Your father wanted a registry office when we got married, you know, but I held out for a church wedding. I said, "You only do it once so you may as well do it right."'

She smiles grimly. 'Will you be going?' And she asks so casually I want to cry.

'I don't know.' That's the truth.

'Oh, you go. Don't want to miss all that free food and booze, not to mention watching Aunt Esther's one glass of sherry go to her knees.'

She picks up the tray. 'Yes, you go. He'll want you there, just as I would. Not that I have any plans to get married at present,' she laughs, 'not even in a registry office. Now, come and be introduced properly to my guests. You'll like them.'

Always talk things out, Mum says. But there are some things not even she wants to talk about. And I know she won't want to refer to the wedding again – or at least, not with me. And I can understand that. For if Adam and I split up . . . the very thought chills me. Not that Adam and I will ever split up. We're going on together for a long, long time, like the rest of our lives.

Wednesday, 20 January:
A Phone Call for Jade

It's just after 6.00 p.m. when the phone rings. It's too early for Adam so I let Mum answer it and I'm just going upstairs to wash my hair when I hear, 'You want to speak to – who?'

Even if it's a wrong number my mum has to get involved. Especially as there's a family down the road whose phone number is very similar to ours. But then Mum exclaims, 'Jade? No, I'm sorry, I can't think of anybody local with that name, but perhaps you –'

And then the phone is torn from Mum and almost out of its socket as I gasp, 'Hello, yes, this is Jade. Sorry about that. We've got a new cleaning woman and she hasn't learnt all our names yet.'

Mum's eyes are body-popping now.

'Hello there, Jade. This is Alison from *Who Do You Woo?* here.' She speaks in a bright yet brisk tone like a dentist's receptionist. Only no dentist's receptionist has ever set my heart thumping as it is now.

'Thank you very much for filling in our application form for *Who Do You Woo?* We would like to invite you to a first interview – we're holding them across the country at the moment. Now, the one most convenient for you, I think would be . . .'

I'm saying, 'Yes, that's very convenient,' before I even hear the full address or the time – this Friday at four o'clock!

'I'm sorry it's such short notice . . .'

'No, no, that's not short notice at all. And thank you,' I gush.

'Now, our interview is very informal. It's simply an opportunity for us to get to know you, that's all. So, on Friday, just relax and enjoy yourself, all right? Well, I'll look forward to meeting you then.'

'Yes, so will I. And thank you very much.'

Did I thank her more than four times? Easily. I must stop that. It marks me out as an amateur. It's just I feel so grateful to them for wanting to see me. And I can't believe it. It's like discovering you've won a thousand pounds. Only better. Much better.

I tell Mum. She's never heard of the programme. She

does say, 'Oh, that'll be good,' and asks what I can win – but she doesn't begin to appreciate the full glory of it all. So I ring up Kay and tell her. We talk for an hour.

Then I ring up Liz who says, 'I didn't know anything about this. Why have you been holding out on me?' and her voice sounds oddly muffled.

I reply, 'Well, life in television is very uncertain and there have been so many tests for *Who Do You Woo?*'

'What kind of tests?' asks Liz.

Showing off madly now I say, 'Oh, written tests, posture tests.' I go on and on making up all these tests (I don't know how I thought of them all) until Liz says, 'And you've passed them all. Why, that's wonderful. I'm so proud of you.'

Then I start feeling pathetic. After she rings off I feel even more pathetic. Not only have I made up a feeble pack of lies but I've let my secret out. Liz could tell someone else who could tell . . .

I ring Liz back, swearing her to secrecy. Only she's already told Mark, who apparently remarked, 'How bizarre.' He also claimed never to have watched the programme but if I give him the date I'm on he'll make an exception in my case.

'You don't know the date you're on, do you?' asks Liz.

I mumble something and quickly ring off. I don't even know if I'm going to be on yet. I mean, I'm just going for a first interview. So presumably there's a second interview, possibly a third or even a fourth!

Typical of me, isn't it, to get all carried away like this? And it's going to be well embarrassing now if I don't get on. And what about Adam? If he should find out from someone else . . . I must tell him.

He pops round for just half an hour, says he's dead tired. I smile at him, open my mouth, gulp hard and then decide to forget the whole thing. It's not fair to tell him when he's so tired. So, instead, I content myself with staring at him and trying to imagine what his reaction will be.

No, I think it's best not to tell him at all. Well, not yet. After all, if I don't get on the programme it'll be just a lot of aggro for nothing. And if I do? Well, like Scarlet O'Hara, I'll think about that tomorrow.

Tonight, all I can think about is *Who Do You Woo?* For this is my chance – perhaps my one and only chance. I just hope I don't blow it.

Friday, 22 January:
You Were Crap

I only remember a tiny fragment of what I dreamt last night. But I know I was on TV. And I recall exactly what I was wearing.

As soon as I get up I put those clothes on again, enjoying the sense of unreality about the whole thing. Then I argue with my mum about coats: I'm determined not to wear one, as I never know what to do with it. I win the argument, only as soon as I get off the train it buckets down. So I arrive at the Leisure Centre dripping and breathless. Guys in tracksuits circle round me curiously and direct me to a large dining room. A woman sits writing behind a desk while four guys all in tracksuits sit around whispering and sniggering.

'Name, please,' says the woman behind the desk to me.

'Jade.'

'Thank you, won't keep you a minute,' she says, still without looking up.

As I sit down the guy nearest me begins calling up someone on his walkie-talkie. 'Come on, Malc! We're all here and about to start.' But Malc is not to be persuaded and I can't altogether blame him. This is worse than a job interview, for at least you know vaguely what to expect then. I haven't a clue what's going to happen in this place, which feels just like a doctor's waiting room.

'Malc's gone shy,' pronounces the guy with the walkie-talkie.

The woman behind the desk suddenly pops up. 'It sometimes happens,' she says. 'Another time, perhaps. Anyway, we'd better make a start.' She has a bright, perky face and is very made up. I can imagine her playing an air hostess in an advert.

'So, introductions. Well, my name's Alison and I met all of you briefly when we came down looking for fresh faces – oh, except for you, Jade. But we had a good chat on the phone, didn't we?' She makes it sound as if we'd been chatting away for hours.

'Well, congratulations on getting this far. You've all done very well. But before we go any further there's something I must explain. We are not a dating agency.

We're a game show and what we're about is having fun. Right?'

'Right,' we all chant.

'Good. Now tonight I want to get to know each one of you in turn for about five minutes. So the best advice I can give you is just relax and enjoy yourselves. The big question is – who's going first?'

I hear one of the guys call out, 'Ladies first,' and I think what the hell – let's get this over with. Waiting around will only make me more nervous.

'Well done, Jade,' she says. She fixes up a running order for the others, then they all file out.

'Good luck,' one of them calls.

Alison places a chair opposite her for me and then smiles at me. Up close, her eyes look tired, very tired, and she seems older. But her voice is mellow, gentle and friendly, and has a definite confide-in-me tone.

She asks me to describe the man of my dreams. That's easy. I describe Adam with more money and a better job and a car.

'Now I want you to imagine the man of your dreams is listening to everything you say . . .' Adam here – listening to me – my blood freezes at the very thought. 'And you want to impress him, don't you?'

I realise I've stopped nodding at Alison. 'Oh yes, yes, I do,' I say quickly.

'Splendid. So, Jade, if you could be an animal, which animal would it be – remembering you want to give an answer to please your ideal man?'

Into my head comes, 'I'd like to be a cat so I could sit on his lap. That would be purr-fect.'

And it's so corny I blush as I say it. But Alison seems quite pleased with me. It is difficult to tell though, as she gives the same encouraging smile to all my answers.

All her questions are more like word games and nothing about the real me at all. I'm disappointed, I admit it, as I don't really feel I've had a chance to show what I can do.

And I decide Alison's smiles are just to make me feel good. Really, she's thinking, This kid's got the intelligence of a jellyfish.

As I'm leaving I pluck up my courage to ask, 'When will I hear anything?'

'You may hear tomorrow,' she says. I let out a tiny gasp which quickly dies away as she goes on, 'Or you may hear in a year's time, or you may never hear. Really, the best advice I can give you is just forget you've ever done it.'

I decode this as meaning, 'You were rubbish.'

I arrive home, defeated.

'How did you get on?' asks Mum.

'Don't ask,' I reply.

Mum makes a cup of tea and generally talks to me like I'm an accident victim. Then, just to add insult to injury, *Who Do You Woo?* starts up on TV.

'This is it,' I tell Mum.

She watches it curiously, then smiles. 'Why do you want to go on this?' she asks.

I can't explain it, not even to myself. I just know my craving to appear on there is stronger than ever. And isn't it funny how every time I see the show it looks better and better to me?

'And what does Adam think about this?' asks Mum. 'I certainly can't imagine him being exactly delighted.' She stares at me. 'He does know?'

I giggle nervously. 'I thought I'd surprise him,' I say. When people act all heavy and intense about something, I turn flippant and silly. I'm a bit pervy that way.

'Jade, how can you go on a dating show without even telling the boyfriend you've gone out with for . . .?'

'One year exactly, tomorrow.'

'Exactly. So, you tell me. How can you do that?'

'Very easily.' I just can't lose my flip tone even though it's inflaming Mum.

'Now, look, my girl, Adam's a nice lad, and he's put up with a lot from you –'

'Oh, thank you,' I interrupt indignantly.

Mum sweeps on. 'But you can't play games with him.

You must be honest, be straight. If I've taught you nothing else . . .' Just occasionally my mum's voice really irritates me. Especially when it rises with indignation and self-righteousness. Like now. Finally, I interrupt her.

'I don't know why you're making such a fuss,' I cry. 'I'm not going to be on the show, anyhow.'

'And don't expect any sympathy from me about that,' says Mum, snatching away my cup of tea before I've finished.

Adam is such a pet of hers, it's almost disgusting. And she's still going on about him now. 'Relationships are just too precious to throw away on a whim,' she says.

'It isn't a whim.'

'Of course it is. That show's utter nonsense.' She marches to the door. 'I think you can count yourself very lucky you weren't picked. Going on that show would have caused you nothing but trouble.'

I wait until she's safely out of the room before I reply.

'No, it wouldn't. Going on there might have changed my life and I bet I could have made Adam understand that.'

Saturday, 23 January:
A Brilliant Evening

For our anniversary Adam orders a taxi for seven o'clock – and won't tell me where we are going. We end up several miles out of town in a tiny village which consists of a white bridge leading over a stream, a white poodle snoozing on the lawn and an old pub whose car park is full already.

As we go into this pub/restaurant, Adam tells me his friends at work had said this was the place for candle-lit dinners. And I have a horrible thought – what do warehousemen know about good restaurants? – which I instantly swat away.

Upstairs is also very olde-worlde with oak beams and copper and iron pots hanging about the place and a huge bookcase with books that have probably been unread for hundreds of years. Yet, it's also quite slinky with low lighting and seats so high they are more like booths.

Actually, there's such a sense of occasion about being here, it's stifling. And we're talking in whispers and smiling so politely at each other we could be strangers meeting for the first time.

Then Adam says, 'Don't get excited, but right by your foot there's 2p.'

I peer down. 'Why, so there is.' And I lean forward and stamp my foot on the 2p. 'It's dead now,' I say. 'Won't bother you any more.' And for the first time that evening Adam smiles naturally.

Then, when the waiter brings over the soup, I whisper, 'He's a really nice bloke but his trousers don't hang properly. Should I tell him he needs a belt? And Adam just cracks up when I say that. Soon everything I say is making him laugh. And by the time the candle on our table starts smoking – well, we're both in hysterics.

Then Adam spots Lanky. He used to teach at our school and neither of us ever liked him for he was permanently furious. If you so much as spoke in his class he'd scream, 'Cretin, shut it.'

'If he ever caught you chewing,' says Adam, 'he'd go, "Stop masticating," and then look all round as if he'd said something really funny. He also had a thing about camels.'

It's amazing to remember how much he scared me. For

now he just seems odd, sitting there all on his own, turning these bicycle clips round on his hand as if they're bracelets and he's totally amazed by them.

As we're leaving Adam suddenly calls over, 'Lanky, Lanky,' just like people used to at school. And Lanky, who knew his nickname, looks all around, so totally bewildered, it's magic.

Outside, Adam and I are giggling away as if we're pissed.

'Well, I think we both totally disgraced ourselves in there,' says Adam.

'Oh, I just couldn't handle that place,' I say. 'It was so pompous and hushed. It was a wonderful meal though,' I add hastily.

As we've half an hour before the taxi returns we decide to go for a walk. We go down some steps on to the bridge and watch the stream frothing away like a mad dog. The view across the stream isn't any better – rows and rows of houses so twisted together they look deformed.

But then we follow the stream deeper into the countryside until all we can see is the sky sparkling with a million stars. We lie on the grass trying to count them all. Or rather Adam does, chanting the numbers like some mad Egyptian priest or something, while the moonlight makes him look pale and slightly unreal – more like an image on a TV screen than a real person.

And I sit there wishing this evening was recorded on film, for I don't want it to get lost. And most memories get lost in the end, don't they? I mean, I can remember a few moments from when I was three, four, five, but only a few and even those keep shrinking. But if tonight were on film – well, then it could never shrivel into the past. It would always be there.

Then, just when I think the evening can't get any better, Adam suddenly says, 'This fell off the back of a lorry. Happy anniversary.'

We'd exchanged small symbolic presents (I gave him boxer shorts with hearts all over them; he gave me an old song 'Never Gonna Give You Up') so I'm not expecting anything else. And certainly not a ring with two hearts – one gold, one blue. They are separate, yet overlap. Two hearts forever entwined.

And it's so beautiful. Only, getting a wonderful present is also rather like being pushed into a freezing cold swimming pool – a real shock to the system. So, at first, I can only gape at him and shiver.

'Adam, I don't know what to say.'

'Well, usually on these occasions people say, "Oh, Adam, it's so beautiful." I mean, they don't all say, "Oh, Adam," of course. In fact, if the person who gave you the ring is called Jim and you say, "Oh, Adam," I shouldn't think he'd be too pleased.'

'All right. Oh, Jim, it's so beautiful.'

'Thank you. Er, have we met before?'

I look at my watch. 'It's exactly a year ago now.'

'No, you're a minute slow. It's exactly a year and one minute ago when I asked you out at that party and you said "Yes" just to shut me up. See, I knew – I knew you weren't crazy about me then. Can't keep your hands off me now, of course. That's why I bought this.'

He hands me a receipt for two rooms in Brighton on 3 and 4 April. Two rooms! I'm almost disappointed. No, I am disappointed. It makes it seem tamer, somehow.

'They're for the first week after Easter,' says Adam. 'Easter was booked solid already. But our weekend will be better – won't be so many tourists.'

'Was it very expensive?'

'Highly,' says Adam. 'I've been saving for ages so we could do it right. I mean, this isn't any of your two-miles-from-the-sea rubbish. No, at our hotel, if you want to go into the sea you just stick your toe, your big toe, out of the window and there it is, lapping about everywhere. Only the best for us, I tell you.'

And, for the second time that evening, I feel as if I've plunged headfirst into a freezing cold swimming pool.

Monday, 1 February:
A Secret That Cannot Be Shared

'Oh, it's sweet,' says Liz and immediately I wish I hadn't shown her the ring. Nothing devalues an object more than someone calling it 'sweet'.

What she really means is that this ring isn't expensive enough to be worthy of a proper, grown-up word like 'beautiful' or 'wonderful' – that's why she examines it as if it's just jumped out of a Christmas cracker. And all right, it isn't wildly expensive but it means something – and that makes it priceless. Can't she see that?

No. I don't think she can. We're having lunch together and I'm not enjoying it because Liz is becoming terribly affected (I'm sorry to slag her off but she is) and she keeps answering me with this deadly laugh in her voice, just as if she's talking to a child who's about ten years younger than her and really very silly, if also sweet.

And every time she puts on that laugh I find myself hating her. Not that it's completely her fault. I'm in a foul mood today as I'm still suffering a mental hangover from yesterday. That was when Mum and I had one of our talks. The topic was my future, so it didn't last very long – no time at all, in fact. And it mainly consisted of my mum doing her 'I'm trying so hard to understand you' sigh and looking pained at everything I said.

And the whole charade was in another stratosphere to me until Mum suddenly said, 'I do hate to see you just drifting about like this. I really do.' And she sounded so upset – I mean, genuinely upset – that I've been feeling guilty ever since. It really is time for me to – as Dad might say – get my act together. Isn't it?

And that's why I'm having lunch with Liz. I'm going to ask her if she can get me a job where she works. So I bury my pride, insert my request and Liz is really quite gracious about it all, even if her tone also suggests she's doing missionary work – saving her best friend from the dole, all that stuff. Still, Liz does say she will definitely make enquiries at the personnel department and then suggests I take a look at her offices now, as they are only a five-minute walk away.

One look's enough to turn my stomach. In fact, next to spotting a Triffid in Stevenage, I can't think of anything more horrific. For Liz works inside this giant glass monster, teeming with rooms that are stacked on top of each other so carelessly you can't imagine anyone ever sitting down and designing a building like that.

'Liz, how can you go in there every day?' I ask.

'What do you mean?'

'Well, it looks so awful. I mean, it's like some monstrous greenhouse . . .'

'Oh, don't be silly, Jen. Buildings aren't important.'

'Oh no? How would you feel about living in a whole town of glass monstrosities like that?'

Liz looks at her watch. 'Look, I haven't got time for this. Do you want to come in and look around?'

'No, thanks. If I went in there I might never come out . . .'

I'm exaggerating my horror (to annoy Liz). But the thought of spending acres of time in there really does stop the blood circulating. I mean, going in there must be like – when you walk into the hall on the first day of exams and can see nothing but rows and rows of desks and then you're directed to row K, desk 7 and immediately you sit down it's as if the rest of the world has crept away, even the exit has vanished – now you're completely submerged by the place. Actually, I've always thought an exam room would make a marvellous setting for a horror story. It's certainly the nearest most of us come to being buried alive.

Anyway, Liz's glass office gives me exactly the same feeling. I tell you, one morning in there would be enough to reduce me to a human zero. But Liz is furious with me. She gives me this really dirty look. And there's no laugh in her voice when she says, 'You can't live in a dream forever, Jenny. By the way, did anything come of *Who Do You Woo?* You never told me.' She knows, of course, if anything had, it'd have been the first thing I told her. And the second. So that's right below the belt.

I just retort, 'I think I'd rather not work than have to spend hundreds of hours here.'

We don't even say goodbye to each other. And yes, I was a bit mean to her. It's just she did get on my nerves at lunch today. Still, I suppose she was trying to help in her way. And she's right about one thing. I do live in a dream. And I've certainly no right to act so superior. At least she's earning her own living, not sponging off her mum. And I really don't want to go on sponging! But what in hell can I do?

I start walking towards Vaughan's. I think I knew all along I'd end up back there. Already I feel like a child who's been playing truant but is now going back where she belongs. And I do belong there. Just why did I walk out, anyhow? Basically because I discovered I'm not such a nice person as I thought. And what sort of reason is that?

I march decisively into Vaughan's, instantly setting all

the assistants salivating. People who stride purposefully into your shops are the kind of customers you dream about. I look around. Ryan isn't there or Gary. I don't recognise any of the other assistants. Shall I just march into the back and knock on Ryan's door?

I hesitate. My eyes flick over the hi-fis. Immediately a boy in a white shirt and flowered tie is standing beside me, his hands behind his back. And he's smiling just as if he's about to produce a present for me.

'Would you like a demonstration?' he says, switching on the hi-fi before I can reply.

'What do you think of that sound quality?' he asks, his voice confiding.

'Actually, I've come to see Ryan,' I say. 'I used to work here and, well – Ryan said to see him if I wanted my job back. So, if you'd tell him Jen is here?'

The boy instantly switches off the hi-fi and the smile and looks as if he'd rather like to snatch back the smile he just gave me. 'Ryan's out all day today – should be in tomorrow morning,' he mutters.

'Oh, right, I'll come back then. Will you tell him I called?'

He doesn't answer. He doesn't hear or see me any more, for a woman clutching a large expensive-looking handbag is steaming towards his area. He's already tracking her when I leave. I'd actually quite like to stay and watch, see if he can make a sale, perhaps even what Ryan calls a 'mighty sale'. Then Ryan would bang this gong – something he only did when he saw 'real selling'. He did it for me the first week I was there. It was pretty corny, really. I mean, banging a gong! But I glowed all that day. I remember that.

I'm tempted to go back and see if gongs will be rung for that sales assistant. But then, shuffling up the road I see this tramp. And everyone's darting into shops to avoid talking to him. Everyone, but me.

'Can you spare a few pence, darling?' he sniffs.

He's obviously got a bad cold, as there's this horrible streak just below his nose. I make to give him some money but then I remember something.

'What's the money for?' I ask. 'It's not for another bottle of meths, is it?'

'No, no, it's for an ounce of baccy, my darling,' he cries.

But is it? I'd hate to think of my money helping to rot his insides even more.

In the end I buy the baccy for him (and a little bottle for his cold) – and the shopkeeper's face is a joy. I mean, he stares at us as if we're Bonnie and Clyde or something and actually escorts us to the door. Afterwards I see him still watching us suspiciously with his face pressed right against the window and he looks so funny I burst out laughing.

The tramp doesn't laugh, though, he just stares gravely at the tobacco. And when I hand it over to him he shouts in his hoarse, gravelly voice, 'You're an angel, my darling.' Then he says it again, 'You're an angel,' still shouting. In fact, everything he says is shouted. Then he sidles off and more people cross the road and pretend to be going into shops, just to avoid him.

What are they afraid of? He's just someone who can't cope with the hassle and pain of life any more, that's all. He could be any of us tomorrow. Perhaps that's why they run from him, too.

I arrive home to find the telephone screaming to be answered. It can't be Adam – he never rings from work. Perhaps it's my school. I have a mild seizure. But then I figure, so what if it is? They've got nothing on me now as Mum knows I'm skiving (I told her during our talk). And besides, I'm sixteen and therefore quite within my rights to skive if I want.

Just to save any unpleasantness though, I croak, 'Hello,' and sound about a hundred and three. Then I add some violent coughing until a voice at the other end asks, 'Is that Jade?'

Instantly I drop eighty-six and a half years. 'Yes, this is Jade.'

'Oh, hello, it's Sue from *Who Do You Woo?* here. We

wanted to know if you would be available for a second interview this Wednesday?'

'Oh yes, I'm available,' I say and my voice starts going all croaky again.

But then she continues. 'This is only a preliminary call to check if you are available should you be needed. We are ringing a number of girls at this time.'

'Oh, I see.' Voice falling further than the speed of light.

'If you are required on Wednesday you will receive a further phone call later today. Now, I need to know when you will be in . . .'

'All day,' I interrupt.

I always forget to play it cool. I just get so excited and hopeful. Only this is dead cruel. I mean, fancy ringing people up to say they might, just might, be needed. Talk about toying with human emotions. The question I hardly dare ask myself is – what if they don't ring me later? Well, that proves I was their last reserve, the one they ring in case there's an epidemic of gut ache or something and they're really desperate.

I then spend the next three hours in a state of sheer agony as I wait for the phone call, while trying to resign myself to the fact that the phone won't ring. Finally, at 5.24 the phone rings again, and there is an epidemic of gut ache because they want me to attend a second interview this Wednesday.

The interview's somewhere in London (don't ask me where – I'll find it) and I will be needed until lunchtime. The girl who tells me, Wendy this time, doesn't exactly overwhelm me with her excitement. In fact, she could be doing an impression of the speaking clock. Maybe she's speaking like that to stop me going over the top or perhaps she just wants to go home for her tea. But nothing can stop me feeling totally chuffed with myself.

Shortly after the call Mum arrives home and says, 'You looked pleased with yourself.'

I just smile mysteriously. This time I'm not telling anyone. For Mum certainly won't understand. And Adam? I'll think about Adam tomorrow.

No, what I feel can't be shared with anyone. Except you.

Wednesday, 3 February:
Earth-spinning News

I sit up most of the night preparing my one-minute audition piece. Wendy said I might be asked to do one and I want to be ready. I sleep for about two hours and wake up to a damp, drizzly, smudged sort of day. Then all the way on the train to London I'm wedged in by fat businessmen who smell of dried fart. Not exactly the way glamorous adventures usually begin in films.

I find the conference centre very easily (i.e. it's so large even I can't miss it) and just inside I recognise Alison, who ticks my name off a clipboard, says 'Coffee will be coming,' and hands me a sticker.

And there, in large blue lettering, is my name: JADE. And as I pin my new name on I feel there's only one thing missing – music. In a film the music would really swell up now, just to underline the point that I now have a new identity. Then there'd probably be a commercial break.

But real life unfortunately has no background music. Or close-ups. It just chugs on and on. And I just sit down next to this girl Maria, who's half-Spanish. She tells me about her room-mate, Sue, who's already auditioned for this programme. Only, something awful happened to Sue. When she opened her mouth no sound came out. All at once I could feel my throat starting to dry up. And it's perhaps fortunate that our chat is interrupted by Alison herding us into the lift. We get out at this small window-less cell with sink-back seats.

This is a screening room and we're shown one whole edition of *Who Do You Woo?* I think I've seen it before. Only this time we're all studying it as if we're revising it for an exam. One girl even takes notes. At the end, Alison says, 'I hope that has helped. It usually does. Now I'm going to have to ask you all to move again, I'm afraid.'

We clamber out waving bags and umbrellas and land this time in what Alison calls the conference room. This room is about the size of a football stadium. One half of it is taken up by this table – the kind you see on television when they have big board meetings – with shiny blue chairs. We are told to sit down anywhere and help ourselves to coffee which we do (one girl asks for tea, twice – both times she's ignored).

Sitting at the top of the table and smiling is this woman in a fairly disgusting orange two-piece. When she stands up to address us all I see she's also wearing these really foul black and white stripy tights. But she has a friendly, reassuring voice, the kind I hear on Mum's radio on Sunday mornings. She says, 'My name's Kate and don't worry, I'm not going to make a speech.' Instantly, we're all grinning away like she's saying something hilarious. For this is surely Boss Lady, the one we must please. By the end of the morning she'll probably know personally every one of our teeth.

She says, 'Remember, you're not in competition. You could all be on the programme or,' she smiles faintly, 'none of you.' There are seventeen other girls, two haven't turned up apparently, and I start counting how many I think are more attractive than me. But I quickly stop. Too depressing.

Kate tells us a few faintly amusing stories about herself. Then says, 'Now, I'm sure funny things happen to you, too. So, how about sharing them with us? For *Who Do You Woo?* is all about people having fun, you know.'

Everyone's expression becomes very serious as they try and think of something funny. Suddenly I remember something . . . 'One night, a couple of months ago my b –' I nearly say boyfriend but just in time change it to, 'brother and I are sitting in my lounge when I hear this deep breathing coming from the back garden. "There's someone outside," I say. My brother listens and he hears the strange breathing, too. So then he picks up a stick and a torch and goes out to the garden, with me not too many miles behind. In the garden the breathing's much louder but we still can't see anything until my brother shines his torch into the grass and bursts out laughing – and there are two hedgehogs walking around each other – with great interest.'

Everyone laughs at this and Kate says, 'Nice one.'

Maria's next, but right in the middle of her tale of the time her dog tore her knickers off the clothes line, the door suddenly bursts open and this elderly woman comes in and plants herself down on one of the comfy-looking seats in the other half of the room. Then she stretches her feet out on the other seats just as if she's relaxing on holiday or something, while totally ignoring us.

Someone giggles. Who is she? Has she wandered into the wrong room by mistake? But then Kate says, 'In case you are wondering, that's Alice, our producer, who's sneaked in.

All eyes turn in her direction. But she totally ignores us and just sits there chewing gum as if she is in a different room to us. Is she the one who decides our fate? She must be, I suppose. Strange to think of so much power being had by such an odd-looking woman.

While on the subject of odd people, the last girl who speaks is called Magenta. She says, 'First I'd better tell you how I've got such a splendid suntan in February,' and describes in agonising detail her holiday abroad. Then she says, 'By the way, Kate, I must own up. I've done quite a lot of TV work, also some modelling, helping out at charity functions, you know the sort of thing. And so I am very used to being on camera. Thank you for your time, Kate.'

Maria whispers to me, 'Isn't she gross? I bet she wins, too.'

Then Kate says, 'I think we're all warmed up. So, now for the audition piece. We're going to be very mean and ask each one of you to stand opposite our producer here and imagine she's the man of your dreams. You can close your eyes if it helps.' We laugh nervously.

'You have just one minute to persuade your dream man to pick you. You can sing, tap-dance, yodel, do anything you like. Only nothing too visual – your dream man can't see you, remember. So, now the $64,000 question. Who's going first? Do I have a volunteer, please?'

Magenta almost runs out of her seat to be first. She stands right opposite the producer, who stops chewing long enough to say, 'Not so close.'

Magenta announces, 'I'm going to serenade you with a song,' and sings 'I'm Just a Girl Who Can't Say No' so loudly she makes my fillings shake. By the end of her song we are all clinging to the table for fear of being blasted from it. I'm eleventh. As I take the long walk to the audition spot, I'm right at the other end of the table. I ask myself why am I doing this? I've no talent. I can't do this.

'So, Jade, how are you wooing your Mr Universe?' asks Kate. She'd been scribbling things down during each act (the producer hasn't written anything down, just closed her eyes a few times).

'I'm only talking,' I say.

'Wonderful,' says Kate. 'And can we have a little more volume, please, Jade? Thank you.'

Then nothing but a deafening silence. So this is it. My moment. My big chance. The palms of my hands are sweating and there is an itching sensation in my throat. I'm going to start coughing any minute. I clear my throat. It sounds like a roll of thunder.

Well, say something, you idiot. And all at once I hear myself talking. It's the weirdest thing, almost as if I've split in two. Two sentences in, I get my first laugh, then another, and each laugh is a shot of adrenalin, sending me higher and higher. It's the most brilliant sensation.

When I sit down, the girls are still clapping and Maria whispers, 'That was really good – so natural.'

I don't remember any of the girls who follow me. I just sit there, still breathing heavily as if I've run in the marathon. I was eleven seconds short of the minute but I think it went well.

And then it's all over. We have to have our photographs taken, sign a form saying if we appear on the programme we won't talk to the press without the permission of *Who Do You Woo?* and also say if we would be able to appear on the programme with only twenty-four hours' notice. We all would.

'Well, you may be invited as one of our pickees or even as a picker. Anyway, I hope to see you again,' says Kate to no one in particular.

Outside it's lunchtime and cold and drizzling. I can't go back home yet. Neither can Maria and a few of the other girls. So we all go out for lunch and have a real laugh together. It's funny how chummy we've all become. We're like girls who've been to school together.

Magenta doesn't join us. She's already late for a luncheon engagement – but she's the main topic of conversation. Shirley, this girl from Yorkshire, does a hilarious impression of her and we all say how we can't believe Magenta's only eighteen.

'I reckon she's twenty-five at least,' says Maria.

By the end of lunch we decide she's almost ready to draw her pension. That's when Maria says, 'I don't care if it's me or one of you who wins, just as long as it's not her.'

We drink a toast to that.

It's after 2.00 p.m. when we finally part and nearly 4.00 p.m. before I crash out at home. I lie on the couch, suddenly dead tired, when the phone rings and I answer it, more out of habit than anything else – never expecting – never in a million years expecting.

'Hello, Jade, it's Alison from *Who Do You Woo?* How are you?' Her tone suggests it has been four days not four hours since she last spoke to me. And then she starts asking me how I would feel about appearing on *Who Do You Woo?* Only her voice is so low-key – just as if she's asking questions for a survey or something – that I think this is probably just another of those calls to prepare you for a possible phone call later.

But then Alison says, 'We'd like to invite you to be one of the three pickees on a show we're recording this Friday.'

And for a moment I'm disappointed. I think I want to be a picker, that's the best role, not a mere pickee. But then I grow a brain. Picker, pickee, they are just simple details. The important, earth-spinning news is I'm about to be beamed into millions of homes. I'm going on TV. I want to yell and cheer and act as if I'm about four (not hard for me).

But Alison proceeds in her calm, ordered way with instructions which I write down. I've got to be at the studio by 2.00 p.m. and I'm recording the show at 7.00 p.m. No, it's not a misprint. I had to write that out twice. Then, just before she rings off, Alison says, 'We'd normally give you more notice but two girls had to pull out of this week's recording – literally at the last minute.'

'And I'm replacing one of those?'

'Yes, you are,' says Alison. 'So you're not going to let us down, are you?' She says it as a joke but only half a joke, if you know what I mean.

'Oh no, I won't let you down,' I cry. 'And whatever happens I'll be there, even if . . . even if . . .' Why did I start this sentence and how do I end it? I suddenly remember something Adam says. 'I'll be there, even if the sky goes out.'

Thursday, 4 February:
Destiny Nods in My Direction

Alison rings up at lunchtime with Friday's schedule. It looks like this:

> 2.00 Rehearsals
>
> 4.00 Light snack
>
> 4.30 Studio rehearsal
>
> 5.30 Make-up
>
> 7.00 The recording
>
> 9.00 (approx.) A party

After the party I'll be driven to the hotel and the following morning, after a continental breakfast, I'm driven home, or in my case to the registry office to watch Dad legalise his lust.

Actually, having Dad's wedding this Saturday is proving really handy. It means the money he sent me to buy 'something nice' for the wedding can be used to buy new clothes for a far more important event. Only this takes longer than you'd think because Alison's given me a list of the camera's allergies: we can't wear anything white, for instance, because it burns and goes see-through. And wide stripes, polka dots and loud checks are also out because they strobe. (I didn't know what that meant, either. Apparently it's when the screen flares up and looks like it's got a multi-coloured rash.)

In the end I buy trousers and a top and I look, from a distance at any rate, really attractive. While I'm shopping I also buy Mum some earrings and Adam a white shirt – he badly needs a new one – and two ties to go with it.

This evening Dad's wedding helps me get away with two white(ish) lies. First I tell Mum I'm going up a day early for the wedding to save all that travelling on Saturday. She looks surprised but doesn't say anything for a moment, then she just goes, 'Yes, why not? Good idea.'

And I thought it'd feel awful lying to her (it always has in the past) but this time it only makes going on *Who Do You Woo?* more exciting and mysterious and more mine, somehow.

The second white lie is to Adam. And again everything works out very neatly. For I'd forgotten that this is the Friday Adam is having a reunion with his old form and old form teacher, Bailey (one of those teachers everyone likes). Two or three times a year they meet up, go out for a meal and apparently it's very chummy.

This evening Adam talks about how, in America, they have a lot more school reunions than us, as well as all those proms.

'But you'd hate going to a prom,' I say. 'Having to get all dressed up and . . .'

'No, I wouldn't,' says Adam firmly. 'I don't mind getting dressed up if it means something – and all my mates would be there.' Then he goes on again about all the good comradeship of school, and what great laughs he had there.

Adam's never got this nostalgic about school before. I sense there's something wrong. And I guess it's got something to do with his job. I know he's got this new boss – Pilchards – who he hates. But when I mention this Adam just marches into the kitchen and puts our tea cosy on his head. That tea cosy is so gross, more like a woolly hat really, that Adam adopted it the second he set eyes on it. And of course, as soon as he puts it on tonight any conversation is impossible, which I think is just what Adam intended.

After Adam leaves I notice he's left his scarf behind. It's not the first time. In fact, he does it so regularly even Mum's noticed. She reckons he does it deliberately to give him an excuse to come back again.

'But he doesn't need an excuse to come back,' I said.

'Ah, but subconsciously he thinks he does,' said Mum. 'Subconsciously he still can't believe his luck that you like him.'

'Really?' I said, so unable to hide my delight that my mum had to say something very sarky. But, even afterwards when Adam left a scarf or something behind, I'd think – with a ripple of pleasure – he's still not taking me for granted, then.

But tonight – tonight the scarf has a reproachful air about it. And that's why I decide not to leave it hanging over the settee as I normally do – but bury it away in the cupboard – until, well, just until Friday's over.

For I mustn't let anything put me off my stroke. Not now when everything's working out so well. I mean, it's almost eerie how easily everything's happened this week.

But then I remember this girl on TV talking about how long she'd been waiting for a recording contract. After years of struggle she said, 'Everything worked out for me, all the pieces suddenly came together. And no matter how talented you are, you can't do anything until fate is on your side.'

At the time I remember wondering, When is fate going to play in my team, and could it please happen before

Halley's Comet comes round again? But now everything's happening so quickly, so easily. Is my luck finally changing? Is destiny nodding in my direction at last?

All at once I feel really hopeful about tomorrow.

Friday, 5 February:
My Most Embarrassing Moment

'Now, don't be nervous,' says Alison, 'and we're sorry to keep you waiting.'

We're waiting to show our outfits to the camera, that distinctly finicky god, who must always be appeased. Alison isn't sure if the camera will like my cream top. And if the camera doesn't like it, then I can't wear it. It's that simple. (That's why I had to bring a reserve top.)

Alison rushes out to check if the camera is finally ready, while my two rival contestants and myself are left alone for the first time that day. Sitting on my right there's Carol. She's a redhead with large green eyes and lovely skin and has been sponsored by a health club to do this. She's also a great laugh. Unlike the girl on my left. She's more of a joke, one of Nature's larger jokes.

Of all the TV shows in the world, Magenta has to pose into mine. And she's convinced she's the dead cert. You can tell that by the way she is lolling back on her chair – it should be a divan – and patting her black curly hair (which is all done up in slides and looks truly awful). And you won't believe what she's wearing. Only a black 1920's dress. And yes, it's an original. (Would she wear anything else?) first worn by her great-granny in 1924. Earlier, light brown snaps of this vintage relative were passed round (actually, her great-granny looks sweet, like a sad bush baby) while Magenta provided a non-stop commentary. 'I'm so happy and proud to be wearing the same dress that my great-grandmother wore during the Roaring Twenties. My great-grandmother said she was always happy when she wore this dress. She died when I was four years old so I can hardly remember her. And yet, I feel very close to her tonight . . .'

And if Alison hadn't been scribbling all this down I knew she'd be applauding. 'Carly can definitely use this,' she says and sends a girl to type it all up. Somehow I doubt the story of my outfit – bought off the rack in Stevenage yesterday afternoon – would have quite the same impact.

At last, Alison returns saying, 'We're ready,' and bustles us to the recording studio. Just before we enter, Alison says, 'Sssh, you must be very quiet now,' as if we are going into a church.

And inside it feels like a church, with dim lights everywhere except on stage and this hushed, talking-in-whispers atmosphere; but a church crossed with a sauna, as it is also stiflingly hot. It's then I notice we are being trailed by three other girls, always keeping about four paces behind us. These, I discover, are our understudies.

'How awful,' I say to Alison, 'to get so near, yet never be able to actually do anything, unless one of us breaks a leg or something.'

'Oh, don't worry about them,' she says. 'Eighty-five per cent of all our extras come back.'

But I can't help thinking of the fifteen per cent who don't.

The stage itself is like a Tardis in reverse, much, much smaller than it looks on television. In fact, the whole studio is really compact. Even the seats where the audience sit are terrifyingly near.

As we walk on to the stage, Alison hands each one of us an envelope. This contains our biography, which we have to check – and our number.

'If you lose that envelope I'll be very cross,' says Alison, then she half laughs.

My number is Three and I think going on last will be an advantage. Magenta's Number Two and Carol's Number One – which she doesn't seem to mind.

Then we have to stand in our number order while

these elderly ladies in black fit our masks. Mine is tur-
quoise blue with gold highlights. It is very shiny and
sparkly and smells like plasticine. It is also surprisingly
comfortable because of the fur on its back. In fact, I really
like it until I see Magenta's mask. She's brought her
own, of course (I hadn't known you could do that), which
is totally black except for silver round the eyes and is
made – so we are told – from over one hundred feathers.
It certainly creates a spectacular effect. Although Carol
remarks that it makes Magenta look like the cat woman –
and to be honest – I'm not sure it suits her. For Magenta's
eyes are very small and too close together, anyway, but
beneath that mask her eyes seem to shrink even more.
Now they look like two rather under-developed cherries.

Then the cameraman says, 'All the boys have caused
the camera problems, so let's see if the girls can do better.'

And all three of us start straightening ourselves up as
if we are going to see the headmaster. Actually, I think
seeing the camera is more nerve-racking.

When it's my turn I stand at the front of the stage and
ask, rather bravely, I think, 'How will I know when the
camera's on me?' This had been bothering me all day.

'You need never look for the camera,' he replies, 'as the
camera's on you all the time.'

I gasp.

'Oh, there's no hiding place from the camera,' the

cameraman chuckles. 'He's the great all-seeing eye up here.' Then he says, 'Now, just relax for a moment.'

That seems an impossible request but actually standing there, bathed in this beautiful pink light, I find myself relaxing quite easily. In fact, I feel really good up there and then the cameraman says to me, 'Yes, no problem. You must be a natural, somehow. The camera certainly loves you.'

He's probably just being nice but I don't hear him say that to the others.

After our audience with the camera is at an end, we're rushed into make-up. It's a bit like the hairdresser's there, with four large mirrors and chairs. Laura, the girl who's in the first half of the show as a picker, joins us. She's okay, I guess, blonde (with dark roots), very loud and confident. But what's amusing is that she and Magenta hate each other on sight. So they keep trying to put each other down while Carol and I grill the make-up girls, Sue and Lizzie, about our picker.

'We've just given him some powder and a little bit of blusher and he liked that,' says Lizzie.

'But what does he look like? asks Carol.

'Well, I'd go out with him. I can tell you that,' says Lizzie.

We try and pin them down to more precise details.

'What colour are his eyes?' ask Carol.

'Brown,' says Sue. 'At least, I think they are, aren't they, Lizzie?'

'Couldn't tell you,' says Lizzie. 'I was so dazzled by his good looks I didn't really notice.'

And at this both she and Sue kill themselves laughing. So we're not sure if they're being sarky. Carol thinks they are.

'Most of the guys on here are really gross,' says Sue. 'There was one recently,' she shudders, 'had a face like a ripped pocket.'

Actually, it would make life a bit easier if tonight's picker does have a face like a ripped pocket. For then, at least, Adam couldn't get so jealous . . .

Adam – every time I think of him today I feel this kick right in my stomach. That's why I escape to the ladies' for a minute. I need to convince myself just once more I shouldn't feel guilty – and it's then something rather strange happens.

Magenta rushes in, doesn't even see me, and then proceeds to start rubbing off all the make-up Lizzie and Sue have so carefully and skilfully put on just five minutes earlier. She demolishes the lovely full lips Lizzie has given her. Now, just a pale slit is left. What is she doing? It looks as if she's deliberately sabotaging her chances.

It's then I call out, 'Caught you. Now I'm going to tell on you.' I mean it as a joke but Magenta whirls round and gives me a look of such undiluted hatred, I shrink back.

Then she cries, 'If you do tell I'll punch you.'

She reminds me of a six-year-old yelling threats in the playground. And she's made such a silly, pathetic, totally inappropriate threat to me I want to laugh in her face; only, there's something about the way she's glaring at me that suggests she could easily lash out, leaving me with a black eye or worse. It's like being faced with a six-year-old suddenly grown to full size and it's quite scary, actually. That's why I say pacifyingly, 'Of course I won't tell. So don't worry.' It's my turn to sound like a kid in a playground now. The one who doesn't want to get beaten up.

Magenta relaxes a bit then. 'I can do my make-up much better than those amateurs.' (She can't. She looks awful.) And then she smiles at me – and that's pretty scary too – before inviting me to come and stay with her. She even gives me a card with her address on. And I take it and say, Yes, we really must fix something up, even though I haven't the slightest intention of going. And we both stand there for ages, talking absolute nonsense to each other out of sheer embarrassment, I think. I mean, Magenta is clearly uncomfortable about what she said to me and for some reason I feel as if I've just witnessed something I shouldn't.

It's actually a relief when Alison knocks on the door to

ask if everything is all right and then tells us that Giles is waiting for our fantasy dates.

I keep forgetting that each of us has to think up our ideal fantasy date. Then the winner has the chance to go on either her fantasy date or her partner's – depending which card is chosen. Last week's winners went to Hawaii – only it was really the studio decked out with a few palm trees and a woman who used to read the news dancing about in a grass skirt.

Of course, my mind goes totally blank about a fantasy date. And I have no ideas at all until I remember something Adam and I were talking about last night – the School Proms they have in America. And I've always longed to go to one of those. So I write that down and hand it to Giles – he's the one with the horn-rimmed spectacles I'd seen before – who reads it and doesn't look too impressed.

But he doesn't say anything, for it's time. Or almost.

We're going to be on the air in just fifteen minutes now, and we are led into this little room off the studio.

'Look at my hands,' says Carol. 'I can't stop shaking.'

I take her hand and squeeze it. 'You're going to knock 'em dead,' I say. Where have I heard someone say that? In some old musical I watched years ago.

And then Carly Carter squeezes in to wish us luck. It's quite a shock seeing him suddenly in front of me, in all his blubbiness, eyes aglow with chumminess. I smile sweetly at him. I want him to be on my side.

After Carly leaves we slide into silence. There's nothing left to say now. Even Alison and Giles have given up making conversation and are just sort of smiling in rotation. Then, from what sounds like far away, although it's actually only a couple of metres away, the show's theme tune starts up. Laura and her three pickees will be out there now with Carly and in a few minutes I'll . . .

My stomach starts doing back-flips, really large back-flips, too, that reach right down to the pit of my stomach. These two ladies in black come in then. And when one of them puts what seems like a piece of string up my top (actually, it's a microphone) she says, 'You're all tense, relax a bit, dear.'

I try and smile at her, only that's pretty difficult when you can't feel your lips any more: my whole face has gone numb, just as if I'm outside on a freezing cold morning. Only, the cold's somewhere inside me, turning my whole body into a block of ice.

Then Giles and Alison start fluttering – Kate appears for the first time that day – and the ladies in black hover in the doorway with our masks.

Carol whispers, 'This is it, Jade.'

But I can only grunt in reply. I think my whole body is about to seize up.

I just about make it to the wings. And I stand there watching Carol being very professional (her impressions are amazing) and Magenta being Magenta, while I start shivering as if I've caught a cold. In a way I have, cold feet. Who said going on last would be an advantage?

And then it's my turn. My legs are like lead now, only heavier, and I don't so much glide into the spotlight as totter. Carly Carter waits with outstretched arms for me at the bottom of the stairs, while the audience clap politely. All I have to do is walk down some steps. And it's not exactly difficult. I mean, a child of two could do it. Only, I miss a step.

Now, I don't topple over and fall on my face with an almighty splat or anything ghastly like that. No, it isn't that bad. It's pretty bad, though. I mean, the audience goes 'Oooh' like they do in circus films when someone drops off the trapeze. For I actually lose my footing and fall forward in a rather abrupt fashion on to my left ankle. After which I desperately try to look nonchalant and casual while Carly wobbles about beside me.

'Are you all right?' he asks.

'Oh yes, I'm fine,' I say and to prove the point I lean forward on to my left ankle. This isn't such a good idea, as immediately several hundred volts of pain go shooting through my body and it's such a sharp kind of pain I let out a gasp. Straightaway Carly says, 'I think you've got a twisted ankle,' and shouts, 'Can we have a little first aid over here?' He adds, 'Never happened before you, you know. Never had anyone slip on those stairs before.'

My one wish is to crawl away and die. Quietly. Only I can't even do that. All I can do is hobble about with a fixed gimpy smile on my face and a steady burn of pain in my ankle. And the bandaging ceremony takes place in full view of the audience, who are fascinated. There's this very tense silence, like the kind you get in snooker finals, while a woman bandages up my ankle. Only, when she says to me, 'That's loose so it won't cut off your blood supply,' some people start laughing, obviously convinced there's a joke in there somewhere.

Then Carly says, 'I was going to chat to you about your most embarrassing moment.'

And I reply, 'Oh, this is definitely my most embarrassing moment.'

Well, the audience wet themselves and Carly gives me a sudden hug, or squeeze would be more accurate. And I'm shocked, not so much by the squeeze but by the great rivers of sweat I suddenly notice on his face.

After my ankle is well and truly bandaged up, Carly asks, 'Are you ready for the one-minute wooing now?'

And do you know, in all my embarrassment, I've actually forgotten about the guy in a highwayman's mask sitting behind a table covered in blue hearts. I steal a quick glance at him then. And he's smiling. I've given him a good laugh if nothing else.

As I struggle on to my stool Carly is gushing, 'She's a plucky young lady, isn't she, folks?' And they all start clapping me as if I've just won a bravery award. You could say I gained more applause for falling over than either Carol or Magenta got for their entire act.

'Your one minute starts now, love,' says Carly, 'and we're all rooting for you.'

And they really are. I mean, I can't help looking into the audience because they're so close. And this isn't a sea of faces as I'd imagined. I can make out individuals. Like in the front row, where this woman is staring at me and really willing me on, just like my mum and dad when I was in that nativity play. In fact, it's almost like my mum is here and all my friends. I start to relax.

And all around me now is the light – warm, pink and protective. I stare into the light, just the way I stare into my mirror at home. And at once the words seem to just bubble out of me. I gain my first laugh at the end of my second sentence, as I did on Wednesday. A second laugh comes almost immediately. A louder laugh than I'd expected, too. And it goes on building until it becomes a huge tidal wave of laughter that's so near I feel I only have to stretch my hand out to touch it.

The applause at the end sweeps me up to the ceiling. No, higher, much higher. And I wish my parents were here to see all this. And Adam. Especially Adam. In the end Carly Carter has to put his hand up to stop the applause. He says, 'Now, the big question is – which one of our masked lovelies will Rupert choose? We bring back contestants One and Two to find out.'

We all stand there in number order just as we'd rehearsed, Carol whispering, 'Well done,' to me as she takes her place. Then Carly says, 'Now, Rupert, you can ask each girl just one question before deciding who you are unmasking and inviting to *Who Do You Woo?*

'Good evening, ladies,' says Rupert – a posh, Hugh Grant voice, but cheeky and friendly with just the trace of a Brummie accent. 'Right. First, Carol – you do some pretty amazing impressions but my question is – which of the people you impersonate is most like me?'

'Well, I can't do Tom Cruise or David Beckham unfortunately,' says Carol, 'so I suppose it must be Prince Charles because,' she adds in a very accurate impression, 'we are both very classy chaps.'

'Ten out of ten for flattery,' says Carly.

Next it is Magenta's turn. 'Magenta, I like listening to music most when I'm in the bath' (titters), 'so what I want to know is, will you serenade me next time I'm in my bath?'

'I'll not only sing to you,' replies Magenta, 'but if you're lucky, I'll scrub your back as well.'

That's quite a good answer (for her) and Carly says approvingly, 'Oh, naughty one. Naughty one. Now we move on to plucky Jade.' He says the 'plucky' as if it is part of my name.

'All I'd like to ask Jade,' says Rupert, 'is, do you fall over often?'

And my answer just ripples out. 'I only fall over, Rupert, when I see someone like you. You could say I've fallen for you in a big way.' Rapturous applause.

'All this flattery,' says Carly. 'Rupert here won't be able to get his head out of the door soon.' Then he pats Rupert on the head. 'All right, my old son, it's decision time. Which one of these talented girls has wooed you tonight? Come in a bit, girls, so we can see all three of you. That's super.'

I miss what Rupert says at first I'm so wound up. But then I hear the name Magenta. And I see her leaning forward eagerly. She looks like a seal waiting for that bit of fish to be hurled its way. I always knew she'd win – she's got winner stamped all over her, plus that story about her great-grandmother.

To my surprise I think I then hear a different name: Carol. And I think, is Rupert doing this in reverse order like they do at beauty contests? And suddenly he switches from Carol to say, 'But I have to admit, I've fallen in a big way for . . .'

That's when the applause starts and I'm thrilled, but can't quite believe it. I mean, I'd have been upset if he hadn't picked me but now he has, I think, will he be disappointed when I'm unmasked?

Carly unmasks Carol, who does a brief curtsey, and Magenta, a considerably longer one, before they are whisked away. And then Rupert stands up, towering over Carly – and I remove his highwayman's mask. Immediately there are gasps from the audience as he is very good-looking. He has short blond hair and large eyes that look both blue and green. He's wearing a black jacket and jeans. I tell you, he could have been in a boy band, except when he smiles. For he has such a wicked, devilish smile. He also has a gap in his teeth, but even that suits him, somehow.

And then the music starts up just like it does every week on TV as he unmasks me. And I think, this is unreal, this isn't happening to me. Then before I know what's happening he's kissing me lightly on the lips and I have this odd sensation like goose pimples, only better. He smiles at me again, that strange, teasing smile of his, and when Carly says, 'Our Jade's all right, isn't she?' he replies, 'No, she's not all right. She's magic.'

And the audience start clapping all over again.

Then Carly plops his arms round both of us and says, 'Now, you've both written out what your fantasy date is, and we've put both your cards in this box. So, who's going to pick out the card?'

'I'll let Jade pick,' says Rupert.

'All right,' says Carly. 'Put your hand in, Jade, and let's see whose fantasy comes true.'

I actually hope I'll pick Rupert's fantasy date, because I think mine is a bit silly. But Carly cries out, 'You are both going to an American prom together.'

'In America?' asks Rupert.

'Yes, in America's fifty-second state, London,' says Carly. 'So, how about a big round of applause for a beautiful couple? Take her away gently now, Rupert.'

Rupert puts his arm around me and we leave to whistles and cheers from the audience. I'd imagined us walking down long corridors together. But in fact, we just go round the corner where we are met by a blank wall and Alison. And we are both laughing at nothing in particular until Alison says, 'Sssh – we're still recording.'

As soon as the show finishes we are led into the party. This is held in the same room we'd been practising in earlier, which I thought was a bad idea. There's orange squash, coke – everyone, of course, keeps asking where the booze is – and dried-up sandwiches. I'm given two chairs, one for me and one for my ankle. And I sit there like some royal dignitary, while people come over offering congratulations and enquiries about my leg, as well as telling me stories about the time they broke their collar bone.

Rupert stands behind my chair, like my Prince Consort and several people say we make a good couple. In a way, I think we do. I feel a bit awkward and shy with him at first. But I must say he is good company. We talk about embarrassing moments. And he tells me how last Saturday he was at this party when he put a chocolate finger behind his ear to eat in a minute or two. Only he forgot about it and the chocolate finger fell right down his shirt where it melted. It wasn't until he got home and his flatmate said to him, 'What the hell's happened to you?' that he noticed this black gooey mess just above his trousers.

This is when I ask him about his flat. He says he bought a flat six months ago with a mate in Belgrave Square. I must say it all sounds very impressive.

For the first half-hour Rupert speaks just to me. Then he disappears and I don't see him for the rest of the party. Not that I mind. It's just that later I see Magenta trying to chat him up and I do think that's rather bad form. I've won him, not her. Then I notice Magenta beam her attention on to Clive, Laura's date from the first half of the show. I must say, Clive seems a strange guy. He doesn't talk to anyone much, just sits there picking away at his skin as if he's still trying to pull off his mask. Perhaps he is – perhaps he'll suddenly pull off his skin. (In what film did someone do that?) And as I watch Clive, I can't help feeling very glad my partner's Rupert.

Later on Magenta and Carol come over for a very strained conversation. I feel so awkward about winning, I burble something totally corny about what a shame it is we can't all win. And Magenta gives me a look which could smash glasses and says, 'Oh, don't worry, we live to fight another day.'

When the party's over, Alison helps me out to the taxi, and is really friendly. She says, 'Don't forget to tell all your friends to watch you next Friday, will you?'

I say, 'Oh, no, I'll enjoy doing that.' And I will enjoy telling them all – well, nearly all.

'And you've written down when we're recording the fantasy date, haven't you?'

'Yes.' I read back to her, 'Monday, 15 February at 9.00 p.m.'

She tells me I can come up the night before if I want. Then she says in a pally, all-girls-together sort of way, 'So, what do you think of him, then?'

'He seems all right.'

She laughs. 'Oh, you're going to have fun with him.'

I'm not quite sure what she means by that.

Just as I'm being helped into the taxi Rupert dashes out.

I hadn't told him I was going because he seemed deep in conversation with one of the researchers and I didn't like to disturb him. But he kisses me and asks for my phone number. Then he kisses me again and says, 'It's been a grin, hasn't it?'

As he waves me off I suddenly notice this huge love bite on his neck. And just for a moment a wave of jealousy surges through me. Then I tell myself how absurd I'm being and it passes – more or less.

At the hotel, the staff are very helpful and this woman puts an ice pack on my ankle. But I think she considers me a bit strange, for she says, 'You've got quite a swelling here and you must be in some pain.'

And I say, 'Yes, I am,' while grinning all over my face. And I don't think anything could wipe the smile from my face tonight. It might even survive Dad's wedding tomorrow.

For I just feel so pleased with myself. And it wasn't only that I won tonight, though that was pretty great. It was the way that as soon as I got on that stage all my nerves vanished and I felt as if I'd at last found where I truly belonged.

How Adam would laugh at that. But perhaps when he hears about *Who Do You Woo?* he'll be a bit proud of me too.

*

P.S. I've just given my heart a quick test and I definitely do not fancy Rupert. He is good-looking and intriguing, with an air of mischief I am not totally averse to. He is also quite rich. But, I suspect, he is a terrible flirt. He has love bites on his neck and is definitely not my type. So, please note, I do not fancy him.

Saturday, 6 February:
A Walking Stick and a Wedding

This morning *Who Do You Woo?* gives me a present –
a walking stick. My chauffeur hands it to me after he's
helped me into the car.

So, at the registry office I make a wonderful entrance.
Dad had given me the money for a train and then a taxi
from the station but he certainly wasn't expecting to see
me emerging from such a flash taxi. And when the chauffeur hands me the walking stick, which I immediately lean
upon very heavily, my dad's smile just falls off his face.
And I think perhaps he does care a tiny bit about me.

'What's happened to my girl?' he cries.

My reply is a beauty. 'Oh, it's such a bore. I fell over at
the recording studio.'

By now my relations are clustering around, too, so I

repeat my reply just to make sure they all hear it. Then hyper-casually I go on. 'It happened when I was busy recording a TV programme last night . . .' Everyone is gaping at me now, hanging on my every word.

And when I tell about my falling over but still going on with the show, my dad's sister, Aunt Rachel, says, 'You're a trouper.' There are loud murmurs of approval. Dad says he is very proud of me and I try (and fail) to smile modestly. And I have a great time. To think I used to hate meeting my relations and positively dreaded their questions. Worse, though, was when I was very little and had to exchange wet, slurpy kisses with them all.

Yet after Mum and Dad separated I never saw this lot any more, they just sent me birthday and Christmas cards of startling dreariness. And I'd totally forgotten what some of the minor ones looked like. So it was quite a shock to discover them, still existing outside my memory. But for the first time, I'm not the slightest bit awkward with them.

And when Dad carefully helps me up the steps I feel as if I'm in one of those family sagas on TV playing the eighty-year-old, frail but determined head of the family. I feel, in fact, like a star.

Did I mention, Yvonne is there too?

The registry office itself is very grim, like a classroom really, with a cabinet, a few chairs and a desk over which the ceremony, such as it is, takes place.

The wedding breakfast – really brunch – is much better. We sit down at this long table sipping champagne and swiftly consuming a delicious ham salad. There's also a band playing romantic music. Unfortunately, my dad and Yvonne get up and start doing a slow dance, giggling and smooching together as if they are out on their first-ever date. I go red with embarrassment for them.

Then Dad says what a shame I've twisted my ankle or we could have had a dance together, too! And Yvonne says, yes, it's a shame – but when I come up and visit in Sheffield we'll go round all the night spots and have a great time then. 'You will come up and see us, won't you?' she asks and she's so eager for me to like her I almost feel sorry for her.

I mean, I hate her for what she's done to my mum. But up close, she's just someone who wears too much powder and has loose teeth. And she is still attractive, I suppose, in a rumpled sort of way. Like my dad, I don't think she particularly likes being middle-aged.

My dad – he's a case.

I watch Dad, his arm around Yvonne, saying goodbye to his guests. And then she whispers something to him and he throws back his head with laughter, clutching her hand as he does so. It doesn't seem fair for him to be so happy, when he's behaved so badly to Mum. But my dad – today, at any rate – is glowing with happiness. They both are. And although I hate to admit it, their happiness does have a kind of magnetic pull.

Dad orders a taxi to take me home and as I leave, the relatives pour round me again, checking what time *Who Do You Woo?* is going to be on. And my dad, who's going house-hunting in Sheffield with Yvonne – the honeymoon comes later – says they'll be glued to the screen next Friday and hugs me hard.

All in all, I enjoy the wedding much more than I expected to. In fact, and this sounds awful, I don't want to go home. I don't want to walk into a house smelling of ironing – it always does on Saturday afternoons – and have Mum ask me about the wedding. Oh, she'll be very brave and matter-of-fact about it, but actually, that only makes it worse.

And there, waiting on the mat, for Mum never moves his precious epistles, will be one of Adam's cards. He'll write, I think I know exactly what he'll write, 'Just a note to say how much I miss you.' It'll probably be scrawled in red pen and there'll be kisses, strange kisses like the X in equations. There might be a mistake, too. Even when writing out one sentence Adam can make a mistake. For instance, after his birthday he sent me a card which said, 'Thank you for making by birthday so special.' You'd think he'd at least have checked it first.

Oh, I know Adam's cards are beautiful and thoughtful

and so very kind but sometimes they seem more like reserve notices. Just like the scarves and things he's always leaving behind in my house. *This certifies Jen is the property of Adam.* But what about Jade, who does she belong to?

STOP! Hold it. I can't believe what I've just written. How can I be so evil about Adam? It must be the fact that my ankle's throbbing a bit and I'm in pain which – no, it isn't. I can get evil thoughts any time – and about the people I really care about, too. In fact, they're often the ones who annoy me the most.

And Adam's really annoying me now. I think it's because I've got to tell him about *Who Do You Woo?* – well, certainly before next Friday. And I'm dreading it so much I feel angry with him already.

Poor Adam, I'm not really giving him a chance. After all, if he loves me – which he does – then surely he'll understand that this is something I must do, won't he?

Sunday, 7 February:
I Am Sorely Tempted

This afternoon, Rupert rings me up. It's a real surprise. After asking about my ankle (now turning mauve and yellow, if you're interested) he asks, 'How would you like to come for a cruise?'

I almost faint with shock. 'A what?'

'A cruise down the Thames,' he says. 'I own a boat.'

'You own a boat?' I say.

'Partly, yeah. It's really small. I mean, if you fart you go forward ten knots. But it's dead cosy.'

Well, I'll admit I am tempted. Sorely tempted. But then I remember I am going out with Adam that night and I can't let him down, can I? So I tell Rupert I have a prior engagement and feel very proud of myself, if a bit sick, too.

And my evening with Adam isn't a great success. I

mean, Adam and I go for a quiet drink and end up being unwilling spectators at this big fight. The moron who finally wins goes, 'I've shown him, haven't I?' There is blood all over him, he's broken his nose and he looks dreadful, while no one knows what the fight has been about, anyhow. And I hate being caught up in something so grubby.

I limp subtly back to Adam's place, and we watch *Buck Rogers* on satellite.

He says, 'You really can't watch *Buck Rogers* when you're eating because you'd spray it everywhere. I mean, this has got to be the funniest programme ever made.' He sits beside me, cracking up at the flares, the acting and the ridiculous dancing in a disco sequence while I'm busy thinking where I could have been this evening. I just hope Adam appreciates the sacrifices I've made for him.

Tuesday, 9 February:
When You Become Famous

I'm growing quite fond of my walking stick, it's such a wonderful conversation-opener. Like this morning, I hobble into school and at once everyone falls on me exclaiming, 'What's happened?' They drag the whole story out of me.

And poor Kay, desperate because Stevie Lee hasn't replied to her last letter, says, 'When you become famous you can ring up anyone you want. You could even ring up Stevie Lee.'

She makes it sound as if I'm about to join a highly exclusive club. In a way, I suppose I am.

You know, going on *Who Do You Woo?* has already made such a difference to my life. For the first time I have something to tell people – and everyone's so interested and fascinated. Of course, I am also asked about what Adam thinks of all this.

'Oh, he's very understanding,' I say.

And, in the rehearsals in front of my mirror, he's either very understanding or very amused. Only, no matter how much I rehearse, my voice just disappears every time I try and tell him!

Wednesday, 10 February:
Adam in Trouble

Adam must know about *Who Do You Woo?* tonight. And I tell myself this so sternly I become scared.

I used to be scared to go round Adam's house because of his dad. He keeps rats in a fish tank in the lounge. Now the rats and I tolerate each other. They stare at me with their jet black eyes but never attempt to sit on my shoulder, as they do Adam and Adam's dad. And I think Adam's dad is trying to convert me into a rat lover, because every time he sees me he'll say, 'Rats are lovely creatures, you know,' and tell me some fascinating facts about them. Tonight he says, 'Rats can't vomit, you know.' He says it really proudly, as if rats have their minds on much higher things. I suppose Adam's dad is a kind of retired hippy. He's got long hair tied up in a ponytail and wears clothes like – well, tonight he's wearing pink checked trousers. He's good fun and I like him but he doesn't exactly kill himself with work. That's why most of the money Adam earns has to go straight into what they call 'the kitty'.

And that's why the house is always so messy. At first I found all the messiness quite refreshing (I hate houses which are too neat and ordered) but now this house is just like some wild, overgrown garden that's been left uncared-for so long it ceases to be anything any more except an assault on the eye. And the nose. The main smell in the kitchen is of ancient spilt jam, although as the plate mountain on the draining board rises closer to the ceiling, aromas waft over from there, too! I'll need to wear a gas mask to make the tea in here soon.

'What we need is a woman's touch.' I whirl round to see Adam's dad behind me.

Now, I can't say for sure he's dropping a hint – perhaps he's remembering his wife or something – but he sure is looking at me hopefully. Yes, he is dropping a hint, isn't he? Well, how dare he! And I want to say something cutting to him like, 'You don't have to be female to wash a plate.' But even when I'm mad at people I still want them to like me so I just laugh nervously and look around for Adam (who's still chasing the rat that stole his pen around the lounge). Adam finally emerges without his pen, and doing an impression of a dead halibut. He's been doing this impression all evening.

In fact, Adam looks so totally fed up I become quite anxious about him. And when we finally escape to his bedroom (leaving his dad still dropping hints about volunteers) I say, 'Now, come on, tell me what's wrong.'

'No, it's all right.'

'No, come on.'

'Nah, there's no sense in depressing you, too.'

'Adam – tell me.'

'All right. Well, you know this toe-rag Pilchards has been giving me hassles at work for ages?'

I nod impatiently.

'Well, today I'd just finished stock-taking when Pilchards comes and gives me a real roasting, right in front of everyone, too. He says my writing's illegible, my time-keeping's appalling and, generally, I am the worst in the place.'

'But that's not fair,' I cry, all indignant.

'Anyway, I got so mad I wanted to shout out my doubts about Pilchards' parentage. But I didn't do that! Instead I whistled really loudly. And Pilchards went ape and gave me a pink report.'

'What does that mean?'

'Well, basically – if I get told off just once more, Pilchards can sign my death warrant. And I'm sure the very thought of doing that sets his thin lips quivering.'

'Is there nothing you can do?'

Adam shakes his head. 'It's exactly like school when a teacher has it in for you – there's nothing you can do. They've got all the power.' He smiles. 'I can't even send my dad up there any more.'

'I'd like to go up there myself,' I say.

'Just to really depress you,' says Adam. 'This guy who started after me – a real slimy toad – got promoted today. And you know how he got on? By crawling and grassing on his mates. There's no other way to get on in that place.'

Adam sounds so bitter and weary I put my arm around him, which he holds on to really tightly. I want to tell him to look for another job, one that's worthy of him this time. And I will. But not tonight. There are times when you want someone just to be there for you. So Adam puts some records on and we lie there talking.

'As soon as I can,' says Adam, 'I'm moving to the Arctic.'

'Why?'

'Well, in the Arctic, evenings can last six months. So you'd only have to work twice a year.'

As I'm leaving Adam tells me how much I've helped him and how great I am. And I'm feeling good until I remember *Who Do You Woo?* I became so involved with what he was saying I forgot all about it. Well, I've got to tell him tomorrow.

I've run out of days.

Thursday, 11 February:
An Evening to Rot Your Insides

This afternoon I tell Mum about *Who Do You Woo?* and she's not, as I'd expected, at my throat with a hundred questions. She doesn't leap in the air and shout 'Whoopee' either. But in her own way I think she is impressed. She certainly gives me these enquiring glances as if she can't quite figure all this out. So, if nothing else, I've surprised her!

She does have a go at me for not telling Adam – I'd expected that – but when I say I'm definitely breaking the news to him tonight, Mum starts bustling about, being helpful. She makes the fire up in the lounge and then sets out all these little plates of biscuits and chocolates giving a distinctly party feel to the room. Some party this is going to be.

The doorbell rings at half-seven. This must be him.

'If you want anyone to come in and referee I'll be in the study,' says Mum, winking at me before going upstairs.

I can't help wishing she was staying down here.

I open the door to Adam, a scene that plays four or five times every week. But tonight it's different. And when I smile at him, I feel somehow as if I'm in a play. I can almost hear the audience whispering, 'He's going to kill her when he finds out.'

We go into the lounge. He stares at all the little dishes of food.

'Is anyone else coming round?'

'No – I just thought you might be hungry.'

'I'm starving, actually, because I missed – but how did you know?'

I smile mysteriously.

Adam likes the television on – but with the volume switched right down and a record playing instead. So I put on one of the records he has loaned me. That pleases him.

'You like that song now, then?' he asks.

'Oh yeah, it's really growing on me,' I say. I don't even know what the record is. All I can hear are my lines for this evening going round and round in my head. If I deliver them well, then Adam might just understand.

I ask Adam about work. Pilchards was away today so there's been a temporary lull at least. And Adam's in a very silly mood tonight. He sits next to me cracking jokes and laughing before he gets to the punch line. I sense he doesn't want to be heavy or serious about anything tonight.

I get up and switch all the lights off except one. It'll be easier telling him if I can't see his face very well.

Adam goes, 'Ooh, are you about to seduce me, he hopes?'

'Er, later, later,' I say quickly. 'First I've something to tell you, something that will make you laugh.'

'Oh, what's that?' Adam leans forward while scooping up a small pile of chocolates. And he looks so innocent, so unsuspecting, I have to turn away.

'Well,' I say, 'tomorrow night you'll see yours truly on *Who Do You Woo?*' Phew! I've said it and it's a relief. There's a beat of silence before Adam replies.

'I suppose that's the only show you could get tickets for. So what was old Carly Carter like then?'

'Adam,' I say quietly. 'I didn't go and watch *Who Do You Woo?* I appeared on it.'

He turns his head to one side.

I start explaining. My voice as bright and larky as Carly Carter's while my only audience looks as if he's just had ten thousand volts of electricity passed through him. Oh,

Adam, don't look at me like that. I should have switched all the lights off. For even in dim light I can see his face blazing with hurt and anger. And when he speaks his voice is so slow and deliberate, just as if he's talking on one of those 'English for Foreign Students' records. He doesn't sound like Adam at all.

'So tell me, why are you going on a dating show when you already have a boyfriend?' Every word he says seems to echo.

I shudder and I try and explain it to him. I repeat words I've rehearsed over and over.

'Adam, I know you think wanting to go on television is just silly and immature. But it means a great deal to me. And I can't . . . I can't turn this chance down. I might never get another chance – and I couldn't live with myself if I didn't go on *Who Do You Woo?* . . . But I'm not being disloyal to you by going on. Please don't think that. It's just there's something inside me which keeps driving me on . . . Please understand. Please.'

Adam stares blankly at me. It's like talking into a black hole. All my words have just vanished.

'Really, what you're saying is, going on a moronic game show means more to you than me. Well, cheers, thanks a lot. That makes me feel really good.'

'No, Adam, that isn't true. It's just I've waited all my life for this chance . . .'

Adam laughs mockingly, then says, 'I suppose every-one knows but me.'

I can almost taste his hurt. Talking to him now is like pogo-ing across a minefield. One wrong word and he'll be exploding all over me. It's best I say nothing, let him cool down. So I don't answer that question. I just stare at the chocolates which no one will eat now. If only Mum would come down – anything to lighten the atmosphere. But instead, Adam gets up.

'Well, I'm going.'

'But you never leave this early,' I exclaim.

'Suddenly, I'm dead tired,' he says.

He puts his black jacket on, the one I helped him pick.

'And my scarf. I want my scarf, too.'

I march into the cupboard and throw the scarf at him. He misses it. Then he bends down, picks it up and arranges it carefully around his neck.

'Adam, don't be like this.'

'Like what?'

'Like this. Look, you've got to trust me.'

'I do trust you – well, I did up to . . .' He looks at his watch. 'Up to ten minutes ago, I trusted you.'

I shudder again. 'Adam, please listen,' and he suddenly stares straight at me. 'Adam, you're over-reacting. I mean . . .' Desperate now. 'I mean, if you think about it the whole thing's really quite funny.'

'About as funny as Christmas in Belsen,' snaps Adam. Then in a quieter voice he adds, 'I think you've deceived me.'

There's so much pain in his voice it scares me. How can I have caused him all that hurt? I hadn't meant to hurt him. But how can I make him see that – short of pulling him into my mind? I don't think I can.

And then it's too late, anyhow. For Adam rushes out, slamming the door behind him with such force, Mum rushes downstairs.

'He'll come round. Give him time,' she says. 'He thinks there's more in this *Who Do You Woo?* thing than there is. And that's your fault, of course,' she adds briskly.

But now I've had time to think about it. I don't think it is my fault. Not all my fault. Adam has let me down, too, hasn't he? All he thought about was himself and his own wounded pride.

And I really thought he'd understand what appearing on television means to me. But he didn't. He didn't understand at all.

Friday, 12 February:
TV *Debut of a Wet Sheep*

At 2.00 (afternoon) I see myself on TV for one and a half seconds. I'm on the trailer for *Who Do You Woo?* There's a shot of me falling over and another of me showing all my teeth.

That's when it really hits me – I'm on TV. I've done it. And I let out this bloodcurdling yell of triumph. (Lucky I'm on my own.)

But then the doorbell rings and I'm afraid it's one of my neighbours popping round to see if I've cut my head open or something. But it isn't a neighbour, it's Liz. And she's smiling at me.

'Kay just told me you're going to be on *Who Do You Woo?* tonight.'

'Yes, yes, that's right.'

'Oh, that's brilliant, but why didn't you tell me?'

'Because – because I thought we were in a mood with each other.'

And that sounds so pathetic we're immediately laughing and hugging each other. Then Liz comes in for a cup of coffee and stays until the next trailer of me appears.

'Mark and I have to go to this boring bank dinner and dance but I won't move until I've seen you on TV first. It's not every day my best friend's on TV. You are going to Clare and Geoff's engagement party tomorrow?'

'Oh, yes, I'll be there.'

'Great. And, Jen – I mean, Jade – is it all right if I tell people?'

'Sure, if you can find someone I haven't told.'

Liz hugs me again. 'Oh, isn't this exciting?'

She's genuinely pleased for me. If only Adam could be like that. I ring him at 6.00 p.m. inviting him to come over and watch *Who Do You Woo?* (Mum's idea, actually). And you won't believe how miserable and boring he is. He says he probably won't come over as he hasn't had his dinner yet. Well, I reply, we can provide food here if that's all you're worried about. But he just sniffs, says he doubts if he'll be ready in time but he'll pick me up at 7.30 p.m. as usual for the pictures.

And to no one's surprise, Adam doesn't come round at 6.30 p.m. It's just Mum and me.

And before I come on there's such a long wait. First there are Carly Carter's jokes. 'I hear the police are looking for a small man with one eye. You'd think they'd use both eyes, wouldn't you?' All terrible like that and Mum says, 'I hope they haven't cut your bit for him.'

Then I have to sit through Laura making her choice of Clive, followed by last week's winners on their fantasy date – a trip to Hollywood, staged in the studio, followed by the longest commercial break ever.

And then Rupert struts on and shakes hands with Carly.

'He's got a good firm handshake, anyway,' notes Mum approvingly.

And now the countdown really begins.

First Carol, then Magenta. And by the time Carly utters my name, my breath is coming out in gasps.

I read somewhere that Bette Davis ran out of the projection room screaming the first time she saw herself on screen. Well, I didn't do that but then I did have the advantage of making my first entrance in a mask.

And my somersault on the stairs looks so dramatic, especially the way the camera pans from me to the audience, stricken with worry. Actually, I think it's slightly overdone.

That shot of me smiling, which I'd seen on the trailers, occurs at the end of my speech and Mum says, 'Listen to that applause. You should be very pleased.'

I am pleased for the girl up on the screen for I think she has delivered her speech well. Only she wasn't me. I was watching someone I knew very well, my twin sister, you might say, but DEFINITELY NOT ME. It's just like when you look at old photographs of yourself. You know it's you – but it doesn't feel like you, somehow.

I enjoy watching Jade, though – until the unmasking. Then it's more bloodcurdling than the unmasking of the Phantom of the Opera. For Jade's face is nowhere near as attractive as I'd imagined. Her eyes are too small and her nose – was her nose really that big? And the make-up is all wrong for her, it's far too harsh. (Perhaps Magenta was right to rub it off, after all.)

And the camera won't leave my face. Instead, it lingers there, showing up fresh imperfections. To be honest, I nearly wept when I saw myself. I'd thought – and certainly hoped – I was far more attractive than that. I mean, I knew I wasn't a raving beauty but I'd always imagined myself to be exciting-looking, in a wild gypsy girl sort of way. So it was rather a shock to discover that, in fact, I resemble a wet sheep. I should have kept the mask on all evening.

But Mum doesn't agree. And neither do all the people who ring up afterwards, including Dad ('I'm sitting here as proud as punch'), Liz ('I thought you looked lovely'), Aunt Rachel ('Why did you give yourself that funny name?'), Kay ('Has anyone famous rung you yet?'), plus, best of all, people who had just switched on their TVs and then received the electric shock of their lives when they saw me. Oh, the phone never stops ringing. It's incredible.

Some neighbours even pop round, too ('We said it can't be') and Mum is kept busy entertaining them – and Adam. Yes, he's here, just. He comes round at half-seven and says he hadn't been able to see all of the show as his dad wanted to watch a film on the other side. So Mum plays the video back for him while he sits slumped in his chair, doing his black-hole look.

We are, of course, too late for the pictures so in the end Adam and I just go out for a drink. And as soon as we go up to the bar two blokes do a kind of double-take. It's really exhilarating.

Or it would have been if Adam hadn't behaved so peculiarly. I know he's mad at me for deceiving him, as he so quaintly puts it – but I just wish he'd have a really good row with me and get this over with. Anything's better than him sitting there like a damp squid.

We haven't been out long, when this group of blokes come over. 'My mate was wondering, weren't you on the telly tonight?'

I lean back. 'Yes, that's right.'

'You were on that dating show. You won, didn't you?'

I smile. 'Yes, I won.'

They scrutinize Adam. 'But this isn't the guy.'

Adam gets up before they can say anything else and mutters, 'Let's go, shall we?' and he clenches his teeth as if he's in a gangster film.

Now, normally I could feel sorry for Adam. And I do admit it's difficult for men when their wife or girlfriend is in the limelight. Who wants to be known as Mr Madonna? – all that stuff. But Adam's been so mean-spirited about tonight. I mean, he's hardly even referred to *Who Do You Woo?* He's acting, in fact, as if it never happened. And he could at least have said, 'You were pretty good tonight,' couldn't he? I mean, it wouldn't have killed him to say that, would it?

All he says is, 'You needn't think I'm calling you that daft name.'

And I reply, 'It's the only name I answer to now.'

He doesn't come in for coffee tonight, either, as he always does. He says he has 'things to do'.

And I say, 'Oh, come on, Adam, don't be like this, don't spoil my big night.'

But he just replies, 'I'm knackered and I'm going home.'

Well, I don't say anything else. I figure if he wants to be all huffy – then let him. But I think he's behaved like a real slob tonight. He also ruined the best day of my life. And I'm deeply disappointed in him, to tell the truth.

But actually it is *very*, *very* fortunate that Adam doesn't come in. For Mum is flapping about at the door and when I tell her Adam has gone she lets out a huge sigh of relief and nods her head towards the kitchen and then gives me one of her disapproving looks before disappearing.

For there, sitting on one of our awful kitchen chairs, is Rupert. Suddenly seeing him there like that makes my heart jump. And after he gets up and gives me a kiss, my heart jumps again, even though I don't normally like being kissed when I'm standing up.

'I've been trying to ring you to tell you how good you were,' he says, 'but your phone's been busy all evening – crammed no doubt with admirers. So I thought I'll cadge a lift off a mate and go and see this new star in person and give her these.'

He hands me a one-pound box of chocolates. 'Oh, thank you,' I say. And, really because I don't know what else to do, I start opening the box and then gape at him in astonishment. There are no chocolates inside. The box is empty, except for tissues and one small piece of paper on which is written, Ha Ha Ha Ha.

Then Rupert, grinning away, hands me a white bag full of chocolates.

'What did you do that for?' I ask.

'Cos I'm an idiot,' he says and his smile seems to fill the

whole kitchen. And I think, I do hope I'm not going to get a crush on you.

We sit and watch the video of ourselves over and over. And Rupert makes such admiring noises every time I come on that I decide I don't look exactly like a wet sheep after all.

Then we sit talking for hours. He tells me he's a DJ. First of all though, he wanted to be a model but he kept being turned down because of a birthmark on his neck. He grins. 'Everyone thinks it's a love bite.'

And I blush, for that was exactly what I'd thought it was.

Then he suddenly asks, 'Have you got a boyfriend?'

'Er – sort of – well, yes I have,' I say. 'Have you got a girlfriend?'

'We finished last night,' he says.

'Oh, I'm sorry,' I lie.

'No, it's been on the cards for a while. Then, last night, I finished it.' He sighs. 'I'm going to see her tomorrow, just to make sure she hasn't done anything foolish.'

'She loved you very much, did she?'

'Probably,' says Rupert with an evil grin.

Should I ask him if he wants to sleep on the settee? I'm not sure, especially as Mum might be a bit funny about it. But suddenly he gets up and says, 'I'd better be going – all right if I ring for a taxi?'

'That'll cost you a fortune,' I say.

'It's been worth it.'

'You don't drive yet, then?'

'Oh yeah, been driving since I was fourteen but I'm off the road for the minute.' And he smiles just as if he's made a joke.

After he's rung for a taxi we watch *Who Do You Woo?* together one last time. Then he kisses me goodbye, says, 'I'll see you Monday,' and gives me the cheekiest smile you've ever seen. Then he's gone.

I've just given my heart another quick test. And I think I may have a tiny crush on him. But my crushes never last very long. (I've had one or two others since I've gone out with Adam. Have I mentioned that before?) So that's all right. Anyway, I expect I'm really just grateful to Rupert for making a great day even more special.

Saturday, 13 February:
The Day I Wake Up Famous

Even before I look out of my window I know it has been snowing. There's that strange stillness and all the usual everyday sounds are muffled and far away.

I draw the curtains, then I lie in bed watching the snow swirl against the windows. I love snow, especially at Christmas. The snow missed Christmas last year but it has actually arrived on an even more special day – the day I wake up famous.

I've been wondering exactly how many million people saw me last night. Are any of them thinking of me this morning? And did any TV producers see me? Might they even now be planning my future?

I used to lie in bed for hours trying to see my future. But instead – well, it was as if I were outside a house, where every window was hidden by shades. So I couldn't see anything. I didn't even know if anything was in there. But now the shades have been lifted and I can see room after room lit up with possibilities. Hang on, my phone is ringing already.

I rush downstairs. It's Rupert. He tells me because of the bad weather he's going to come down on Sunday night rather than Monday morning to record our fantasy date. And I say but he only lives about ten miles away. He replies if they've offered to put him up in a top-class hotel why should he say no? You've got to grab everything that's going.

Then he suggests I come up early as well and then we can have a meal together tomorrow night. I protest feebly, saying I'd already spoken to Alison on Thursday and told her I'd be coming up on Monday morning. Still, she has given me a number to ring if I change my mind and the weather is a good excuse – and a night in London with Rupert – well, that sounds pretty good, doesn't it? Certainly more exciting than an evening round Adam's house full of rats and unwashed dishes and Adam being all moody.

Adam and I are barely talking now. And this evening we walk to Clare and Geoff's engagement party in total silence. But as soon as I walk into the party there's a real buzz around me. In fact, I'm almost mobbed. Everyone, it seems, has questions about my fall, my new name and Rupert, of course. One girl says she didn't think I smiled enough but everyone else is full of praise for my TV debut. And would you believe, some people even come over to be introduced. One girl says to me, 'I just wanted to see you in real life.'

Even Mark is quite nice to me. In fact, he insists on dancing with me, something he's never done before. And while we are dancing he invites me to his house for dinner – something else he's never done before.

Then I see Adam scowling in the shadows. I do feel a tiny bit sorry for him and so I go over and get him to dance with me. I say, 'All this fuss is incredible, isn't it?' really hoping that he'll see how happy I am. But he doesn't even answer me, just makes this curious tight sound in his throat. And I can see the resentment just boiling up inside him.

He disappears again when a girl from my old form comes up to tell me how amazed she'd been to see me on telly and how all her family thought I was 'super'.

I tell you, the fuss and attention I received that evening was unbelievable. I reckon I was paid more compliments at that party than I've received in the rest of my life. Perhaps that's why I could have stayed there all night but Adam insisted on leaving early and, despite everything, I didn't want him to be seen leaving on his own. So I leave too.

Outside the wind is cold and heavy. Usually Adam and I would be wrapped so tightly together that I'd be able to feel his breath on my cheek. But tonight we walk a mile apart from each other. And I can't handle this deep-freeze treatment any longer. That's why I almost enjoy telling him about me going up to London early. At least now I'll get a spark of feeling out of him.

But, instead, his face breaks into a sneer. 'I suppose Rupert will be there.'

'Yes, I expect he will.'

'When I saw that guy yesterday I wanted to put a pitchfork through the screen.'

'Why?' I ask, actually wanting Adam to realise some of his feelings.

'Why? Cos he's a smarmy git, so oily and slippery and with such a big ego on him he . . .' He goes on slagging off Rupert and I don't stop him. Let him get all this jealousy off his chest. But then he asks, 'So when does all this bullshit end?'

This takes me by surprise. I hadn't thought of it ending.

'Well, I'm back recording this Monday . . .'

'And that's it?'

'I don't know.'

'It must be. Even you can't make a career out of going on brain-dead game shows, can you?'

I bristle furiously. 'Adam, last night I was beamed into

millions of homes, so who knows what will happen now. You saw what happened at the party tonight.'

'Yeah, I saw all right. I saw you making yourself into a joke.'

'No, no,' I cry. 'That's not true . . .'

'Yes, it is. On that show last night you were just a puppet. Come on, do your little talk then . . .'

'No, Adam, don't.'

But he doesn't even hear me now as he rages on and on. 'And worst of all was the way you smiled when you saw HIM and went on and on smiling, your face all lit up like you'd just seen the second coming or something. When I saw that bit I wanted to go out and be sick in the street. I couldn't believe how you'd degraded yourself. It's going to be a long time before you live this down.'

For a moment I can only breathe in the dead air which surrounds us. I just can't believe that Adam of all people could be so vicious, so nasty, so determined to make me feel like nothing. Then all at once anger – red hot anger – sweeps out of me.

'You can't bear it, can you? I've gone out and had a go at something and you just can't bear it. Well, at least I had the guts to appear on television.'

At once he starts laughing, a cruel, bitter laugh.

'Oh, yeah, go on, sneer, that's all you can do, isn't it? But why not take a look at yourself, stuck in a dead-end job because you haven't the guts to try anything else. You moan and whinge about things but you never try and change anything – no – all you do is criticise other people. Well, I think you're the joke, not me.'

There's no laughter now – instead, Adam turns away from me. And he's shaking. We both are. But I'm too churned up to trust myself to speak any more. So instead, I walk away from him and up the road to my house. He doesn't follow me. When I get in I wonder if he'll ring me to apologise.

But he doesn't. Not that I want to speak to him. And really, I don't know what's going to happen to us now. Tonight was so ugly and so full of hatred. I mean, I hate Adam now, I really hate him. And not because he was jealous – I expected that. But for the way he tried to steal my moment of glory away from me. It may not have seemed much to him but that doesn't give him the right to snatch it away, does it? No one has the right to do that to you, have they?

I think it'll be a long time before I can forgive Adam for tonight.

Sunday, 14 February:
An Ending – and a New Beginning

Adam rings me just after lunch and starts by saying, 'Happy Valentine's Day! Could I bring your present round later?'

I have a present for him, too, but I don't say anything.

Adam breaks the awkward silence by saying, 'I was out of order last night.'

'Yes, you were,' I say.

Then there's another silence. Normally I'd drop in a helpful laugh or make a silly comment. I always feel obliged to fill in the gaps. But today I don't – I let him suffer. But then his tone changes and – you won't believe this – he says, 'I don't want you going to London this evening to meet this bloke. You're to go into London tomorrow morning.'

'Adam,' I say, 'I've already explained why I'm going in early – because of the weather.'

'No snow is forecast for tonight,' he replies. 'All the roads are clear, all the trains are running. So you're not to go, right?'

I am more amazed by this sudden order than angry. 'Adam, if I want to go into London tonight then I will,' I say, quite calmly.

But Adam's tone is anything but calm. 'All right, go and see him but don't come crawling back to me afterwards.'

'I don't crawl to anyone,' I say. And his words don't upset me like they did last night. Now they are just an irritant I want to brush away. 'I think this conversation is at an end,' I say, 'and please don't ring me again until you've sorted yourself out.'

For Adam sounds so strange this afternoon. His voice is all slurred and out of control as if he's drunk. Only, I don't think he is drunk, which makes it worse.

'If you go and see this bloke tonight we're finished,' he yells.

'All right,' I say, still very cool, 'we're finished.'

There's a pause, then the phone clicks off.

I slam the phone down, too. And then I stare at it, numb with disbelief. After going out together for over a year we finish in less than a minute. But, no – we can't end like this. I start to cry. I really don't want to. But I can't stop myself until I hear Mum returning from coffee at Angela's (one of her best friends). And immediately I rush upstairs. I don't want Mum to know Adam and I have finished. She'll only have a go at me. And the whole thing will be completely my fault, of course.

'You were deceitful,' she'll say. 'So what else can you expect?' Then she'll add, 'Poor Adam.' If only she'd say, 'Poor Jade,' just once in a while.

So I dart about upstairs, finishing my packing. When I come down with my cases, Mum is already hidden behind a layer of smoke.

'Angela saw you on TV on Friday,' she says. 'Wanted to hear all about it. Thought you were most professional . . . Are you all right? You look a bit flushed.'

'No, I'm fine. Just excited. Mum, will it be all right if I go a bit earlier than we'd planned?'

'How much earlier?'

'Well, like now.'

'But you haven't had any lunch and Alison didn't say they would pay for lunch.'

'I couldn't eat a thing.' I just want to go, be doing something, anything to stop me thinking.

Mum prepares me some sandwiches, makes me promise I'll eat them on the train and also gives me ten pounds extra spending money which is pretty generous of her.

The train itself is practically empty this time but it keeps stopping and there's a horrible smell of rubber. By the time I arrive at the hotel I'm feeling pretty low again. Alison is there to meet me. She is quite friendly and asks about my ankle (now healing up but still changing colour – it's currently pale lemon). But I think she gives me a rather strange look when she says, 'Please don't abuse the hotel, will you?'

I'm not quite sure what she means by that.

After saying she'll see me tomorrow morning at ten sharp she disappears. The hotel is very posh but also very hushed and musty with an elderly lift that wheezes and rattles as it cranks up to my floor.

I sit in my hotel room. It's large but very impersonal. I feel suddenly very alone. I start to unpack, then I sit down again and look at the ring Adam gave me . . . two hearts forever entwined. I should fling it away now, that's what they're always doing in films. But I don't. I can't. Not yet.

My thoughts are interrupted by the high-pitched screaming of the telephone. For one moment I think it's Adam – he's traced me here and wants to apologise. But it isn't Adam, it's this guy with such a heavy Italian accent I can't understand what he's saying at first. Then I discover this is the assistant manager telling me I've been given the wrong room and I have to pack and meet him downstairs at once.

Well, luckily I haven't unpacked much but it's still annoying – and my bags are heavy. I stomp furiously out of the lift and bump straight into Rupert. I start telling him how I've been messed about but then stop – there's something in his eyes. And all at once Rupert starts babbling away in a heavy Italian accent.

And I feel such an idiot standing there, especially as one of my tops is hanging out of the case, I'd packed it so quickly. But Rupert keeps grinning at me like a naughty schoolboy and in the end I'm laughing, too. Then he says, 'You don't want to eat here in Fossil Valley, do you?'

And he takes me to this restaurant off Covent Garden and it's a dream of a place: fresh flowers, gentle candle-light, American waitresses who are really welcoming and huge plates of food – I loved it there.

I tell Rupert a little about Adam and me finishing. He doesn't seem at all surprised.

'When you become famous,' he says, 'you lose some friends. There's this mate of mine who's been avoiding me since Friday and I know why. Jealous. It's the price of fame. Still – it's better than the alternative.'

'What's that?' I ask.

'Being a nobody,' he says. 'You know, the kind of person who spends their days in some supermarket stacking shelves and saving, "No, sorry, we haven't got any of those in stock." You're either a somebody or a nobody and I've always wanted to be a somebody. And as I haven't got a business brain and I'm not sports-minded I decided I had to get on TV.'

'You want to be an actor, then?'

'No, a DJ I've done quite a bit already in the local clubs and discos. Actually, I'm really good now at getting an audience warmed up. You see, I make them laugh and tease them a bit. And I can always get an audience dancing. Not sounding big-headed or anything, but I'm probably the best DJ for miles around here. But if you're not on TV no one knows you exist. You know what I mean?'

'I know exactly,' I say. 'I want to leave my mark, I want to be –' I hesitate.

'Be loved,' says Rupert gently.

'Yes,' I say, 'be loved. You know, I'd rather be famous than anything else, wouldn't you?' He nods enthusiastically. 'And I want to have a biography written about me,' I cry.

'I think,' Rupert says, 'you've got inside you what I've got inside me.'

After the meal we go for a walk and I am amazed at the number of shops that are still open. Rupert says many of them stay open until midnight.

We are ages in this record shop (not surprisingly,

155

Rupert knows a lot about music) and Rupert whispers, 'What do you know, we're on TV again,' and he points to this guy on a stool who has his face about one centimetre away from this close-circuit television. This rather unnerves me, actually and when, as we leave, someone touches me by the sleeve, I let out a gasp.

But it's a guy in a smart jacket. 'You were on the telly,' he says.

'Yes,' says Rupert. 'We were both on *Who Do You Woo?* on Friday.'

'That's right,' says the guy as if he's been testing us. 'We thought it was you.'

Two other girls, one clutching a boy of about six, join us. Rupert is wonderful, immediately putting them at their ease. I begin to enjoy myself, too. And we chat to them for several minutes.

Afterwards Rupert says, 'Did you catch that jacket? It's a mark-down, I can always tell.'

As we walk down Piccadilly Circus these guys outside one of the pubs start humming the *Who Do You Woo?* theme tune and wave at us. And before we reach Eros we are stopped twice more and each time what makes it special is the shine in people's eyes as they recognise us. Usually people are only this friendly at Christmas and, with the snow gleaming on the paths, this feels very like my own personal Christmas. In fact, if we'd suddenly bumped into carol singers I wouldn't have been too surprised.

'I bet we could walk in any street in England tonight,' says Rupert, 'and people would know us.' And he suddenly lifts me up into the air. 'We've done it, Jade,' he cries. 'We're famous.'

Monday, 15 February.
The Monday-morning Prom

As soon as I arrive at the studio this morning I'm hustled into a changing room. Waiting for me there is one of the elderly ladies in black I've met before.

'Your dress is all ready,' she says, just as if I've ordered it weeks ago. But as soon as I see it, I fall in love with it. It's a pink prom dress exactly like the ones they wore in the 1950s. The dress has two thin straps, a big white belt and is gathered at the waist so it really flares out. It even has an underskirt to help it swing when you move.

While I'm changing Rupert knocks on the door and my dresser says in a shocked voice, 'You can't come in when your young lady is getting dressed.' And she sounds so sweet and protective I want to hug her.

Next she hands me my white gloves. I could be going to a royal garden party, only I doubt I'd be wearing white ankle socks there. Finally she pins on my corsage. (I love that word, corsage, it should be the name for a very expensive perfume.)

Then she opens the door to Rupert and says, 'Now you may come in and see your young lady.'

Rupert is obviously highly amused by this but he bows his head to her and says, 'Thank you, ma'am,' so gratefully I nearly burst out laughing. Only I'm glad I don't – as that might have broken the spell. Rupert looks so smart in his grey suit (like most men he's at his best wearing formal clothes). And I notice again just how good-looking he is. He offers me his arm and the dresser says to me, 'You look lovely, my dear.'

And I think how gloriously unreal this is. I mean, here I am, all dressed up at half-past ten on a Monday morning to go to a prom in a television studio.

Unfortunately they are shooting Laura's fantasy date – a trip to the sixties – first. So Rupert and I have to sit with Giles in this draughty room drinking vile coffee out of a machine – and wait. Only, Rupert can't sit still. He keeps disappearing, leaving me to make strained conversation with Giles.

I even see Magenta briefly. She doesn't let on she's seen me though. And I think how sad it is that even though she's lost she's still turning up. In fact, I almost feel sorry for her.

I wait there for two hours and it feels like twenty. And no one even bothers to tell us why we are being kept waiting so long. But finally, we are on the move. First, though, I have to go back to my dressing room to have the microphone fitted up my dress, which makes me look as if I've got a funny hip.

Inside the recording studio are cameramen setting up in one corner, a group of dancers – the girls wearing dresses similar to mine – rehearsing in another corner, while right across the studio a huge mural of teenagers in 1950s rock 'n' roll poses is being set up. The colours are bright and eye-catching but the actual pictures of the teenagers are pathetic. In fact, they look just like the drawings you see outside ladies' and gents' loos.

I stand about feeling more than a bit lost, especially after Rupert spots the girl who interviewed him and goes over to talk to her. And the only person to even acknowledge my existence is a small guy in green flares and a frizzy blond wig which makes his head look considerably larger than his body. At first I think he's a leftover from the sixties sequence. Actually, he's the director.

'Getting excited?' he says.

'Oh yes,' I gush.

'Splendid,' he says. 'Well, it won't be long now.' Then he scuttles off while I sit in the corner watching Rupert talk to Kate. I must say, he does tend to grovel round authority – something he learnt at public school, no doubt.

But at last the director calls for silence and says, 'The dancers have to leave at 2.00 p.m. so we'll film their part first.'

Everyone has to stand on their marks and Rupert and I are told just to watch at first. The catchy tune 'C'mon Everybody' blares out and all these dancers start jiving and whirling each other about.

Rupert and I are told to clap our hands and sway around, too.

'That's all you've got to do,' says the director. 'Easy, isn't it?' But we've only just started when he puts his hand up. 'Jade,' he calls. 'Can you try and sway in time with the music?'

'I thought that's what I was doing,' I mumble, hoping I'm not turning bright red.

We start up again, only now I am so self-conscious the director stops everyone again and calls across, 'Can we have a little smile, Jade – please?' And in a tone of voice which suggests his dearest wish is to take a chainsaw to me. After we finish that sequence there's more hanging about. And I think, I'm not enjoying this at all. But then, this isn't really my fantasy date, is it? In fact, I'm pretty unimportant in all this, just a tiny piece of a giant jigsaw. And it's all very well the director going on at me to smile but how can I when I don't feel anything? I mean, there's no atmosphere here at all. This is just a conveyer belt – take off the sixties mural – bring on the fifties one. And I'm an artist. I need to feel something before I can show it.

It's then I notice a figure slumped across about four chairs. Can this really be Carly Carter? Well, he must be ill, for his face looks so vacant, so empty, totally drained. And when the director calls him I watch Carly get up, re-arrange his stomach and stumble over to the camera. Something must be wrong with him. But as soon as Carly faces the cameras it's as if a red light has gone on and he sheds about twenty years (so now he looks about eighty). Rupert reckons Carly's just been preserving his energy – he says a lot of stars do that.

Watching Carly is fascinating, especially seeing him read off the autocue. The autocue is really just the script put on a TV screen which follows Carly about. Wherever he goes his autocue goes too. I can't remember exactly what he reads aloud but I can remember some of it (which is more than Carly Carter can) because I like the words.

He reads, 'The High School's Prom is an important point in a young person's life. It's when that person changes from being a teenager into adulthood and they have a final dance before leaving school.' Then Carly switches from his slow, sincere tone into his 'I'm so wacky' one as he yells, 'So come on, let's join Jade and Rupert at the prom.' Then he waddles off, while I notice how small his feet are, like a child's feet really.

Next, it is over to us again. Rupert and I have to do a slow dance together as the cameras move in on us, closer and closer. The old song 'Only You' begins and Rupert repeats the words, whispering them down my ear. And then he starts holding me tighter and tighter. Adam doesn't dance much so it's been quite a while since anyone held me this closely. And yet, this is so easy, so natural – and so arousing. I mean, I am getting really turned on. And I don't get turned on that often, to tell the truth, but my hormones are positively sizzling. And when Rupert kisses me it's as if his body just flows into mine.

The rest of that dance is already a daze. I know they play the tune twice, at least. But actually I just forget about the cameras and the people whispering behind them until the end when the director says, 'All right, time, or am I going to have to throw a bucket of water over you?'

I think that is meant to be funny. Then the director hands Rupert a gold chain with a little card. Rupert reads from the card, 'This gold chain contains my ring. I'd like you to wear it round your neck.' He places the chain round my neck and then kisses me full on the lips.

'Hey, that's not in the script,' calls someone.

Carly then returns and reads, 'We have one last surprise for you, Jade. Rupert knows all about this but you don't.

Lead her to the surprise, Rupert, and I'll see you both in a sec, all right?'

One of the cameras follows Rupert and me down the studio. 'What's happening?' I whisper but he just grins mischievously.

I watch two men slide out this dazzlingly white throne. And beside the throne is placed a carpet of flowers, plastic ones, while some large banners are strewn over the throne. The banners say, 'Queen of the Prom'.

'You have been proclaimed Queen of the Prom,' cries Rupert, 'so will you take your place on the throne?'

He steps back and I am about to step forward when Carly Carter says, 'Not yet,' and flings a red cushion on to the throne. 'Now you may sit down,' he says.

I am so flustered by this sudden outbreak of gallantry I don't spot who's standing behind us.

'To crown you Queen of the Prom,' says Carly, 'we have that king of the teenage heart-throbs – and don't forget his second single is released next week – MR STEVIE LEE.'

Immediately I let out a cry which must sound as if I really like Stevie Lee but actually it is just the shock of suddenly meeting him again like this.

'Jade, I am very honoured to crown you Queen of the Prom,' he says and gently places a gold crown on my head.

'Thank you, sire,' I say and wave my hand to the crowd. I add, 'And thank you, my people.'

'That's good,' says the director. 'Do it again.'

I give an especially regal wave in his direction. I hope he realises now that I can be very good if given a chance – and no one panics me.

And Rupert and I are filmed with our arms round each other. No one needs to shout 'Smile', as our faces just naturally explode with joy.

'Nothing can stop us,' whispers Rupert to me. 'This is our time.' And I realise that for once I'm not looking forward to being happy, I am happy right in this moment.

The final shot is of me kissing, first Stevie Lee – his breath smells, that awful stale smell which means bad teeth – and then Rupert, much more satisfying. Afterwards, Stevie Lee gives me a signed copy of his new single for Kay, even though I don't think he really remembers her. And before he leaves he says, 'Good meeting you, Jade, see you again.' And considering the last time we met he'd only tilted his head slightly in my direction, I can't help feeling a little chuffed. For now we are chatting together as equals.

Then Carly joins us, beaming one of his huge, unfocused smiles across the room. And I realise with a little gasp of pleasure that I'm standing next to Carly Carter. All right, he's not one of my favourites but he is a star, one of TV's biggest. And to see Carly Carter actually existing beside me is fascinating. I ask Carly if he'd mind autographing my diary.

'I'll sign anything but cheques,' he quips. He fills one page of my diary with his huge signature. I want to ask him about getting on to television but Rupert gets in first.

'Jade and I would like to appear on television, like you, Carly,' he says.

Carly makes a face, then he says, 'In this business – anything is possible. I mean, if an ugly mug like me can fill a TV screen every week, well, like I say, anything is possible – and good luck to you both.' Before we can ask him anything else he says, 'Well, I must love you and leave you. So be lucky, now.'

'I was hoping he might have had a drink with us,' mutters Rupert. 'Help us make some contacts.'

And it's not only Carly who's rushing away. Behind us my throne is dismantled and the mural is being carried off, both with unseeming haste, I feel. In fact, it's all a bit like one of those fast-food stores – only they're serving up dreams here.

I can't even keep the dress.

'No chance of me buying it, I suppose?' But the dresser just shakes her head sadly. And as I put on my normal clothes, this awful feeling of emptiness takes hold.

Then Rupert is at the door. 'I told Alison you wouldn't want a taxi home until this evening.'

I open my eyes wide. 'Oh, what are we going to do, then?'

He looks at me in surprise. 'What else? We're going to walk round London and see how often we get stopped in the street. So hurry up, we mustn't keep our public waiting.'

We leave together, hand in hand, ready to greet our public once more.

Wednesday, 17 February:
Letter From a Gerbil Freak

'And just before I kissed Stevie Lee, these girls come rushing up with powder puffs.'

Kay nods. 'Stars must always look their best. Go on.' She wants to hear every little scrap of information I can give her about the day (and especially Stevie Lee). And I know she's hoarding away everything I say for later, when she's on her own.

We're walking through the shopping arcade, just up from my house. And I haven't been stopped by anyone. I think it's because we've had another fall of snow and people are too wrapped up to see me clearly. But I did want Kay to view my fame in action, as it were. So we go into the greengrocer's and there's a mini-riot. It's incredible.

First of all Mrs Almond, who serves there, calls out,

'So, we'll all have to call you Jade now. Won't answer to Jennifer any more, will you?'

'That's right,' I say.

Mrs Almond adds knowingly, 'You were pleased with your choice, weren't you? I could tell.'

Then this woman comes up and says, 'Sorry, I was eavesdropping but I thought I knew you from somewhere,' and starts telling me about the time she went on holiday and won a talent contest. Then I nudge Kay as just about everyone in the shop gathers around and even those who haven't watched the programme want to know 'what it was like'. I feel a bit like an explorer, returning from a magic kingdom. When I finally leave – no time to buy anything – this woman says, 'It's really cheered me up, meeting you.'

Outside Kay is incredulous. 'But it's incredible, the way people just came up to you, as if they know you.'

'You should have been in London on Monday. Rupert and I were stopped so many times. And everyone was so pleased, so excited to see us. One girl said, "See you, then," to us as if we were already old friends. And that welcome makes you feel so confident, so strong. Oh, I can't tell you what a marvellous feeling it is.'

Kay comes home with me – I think she's as excited as I am – and there, waiting on the mat, is a letter. Almost instinctively I assume it's from Adam. But then I see the

London postmark. And it's from the *Who Do You Woo?* office passing on two fan letters received yesterday, with a little note warning me against giving out my address.

'Fan letters already,' gasps Kay.

We read them together. The first is from a boy in Birmingham who sends me a picture of himself from a photo booth; he looks about nine. The other is also from a boy, Bill, but one who lives much nearer, Welwyn Garden City. He sends me a photo not of himself but of his gerbil. In his letter he tells me his gerbil is nearly five years old and is called Tony. He ends his letter, 'Lots of luck with your career.' Bill says I look a lot like his older sister who lives in Australia now. I guess that's why he's writing. And his letter is so sweet, they both are – even though I'm slightly disappointed that all my fan mail so far is from people still at middle school. Still, fans are always welcome and Kay goes, 'Let me touch you. You're a star now.' She's fooling about but she is also really impressed. Especially as while she's having coffee I receive two phone calls – one from Mum's local paper requesting an interview and the other from the local radio wanting to do an interview, just an hour before my second TV appearance this Friday.

Kay really doesn't want to leave and in fact she stays until Mum gets back. 'I'd really love to meet Rupert,' she says at the door, 'having seen him on television and all.'

170

'Well, next time he's down,' I say, 'I'll give you a ring.'

I don't tell Kay that Rupert was supposed to come down today but at the last minute he had to cancel because something unexpected came up. He didn't even ask to speak to me, just left a message with Mum.

I wait for him to ring this evening. And while I wait I answer my fan mail. I end up writing long letters to both. And Rupert doesn't ring. That rather depresses me. So, to cheer myself up I decide to post letters to my fans and see if any of my public are about.

Thursday, 18 February:
Rupert's Private Question

Rupert finally rings at 7.00 this evening. I always knew he would. But just to show I think he should have spoken to me personally on Tuesday before cancelling, I say, 'Oh, good of you to ring.'

'Now, we don't want any of that,' Rupert replies in a voice so heavy with amusement it just annihilates completely my sarcasm. 'Look, I'm on a pay phone so I've got to be quick. I want to see you. What are you doing tomorrow night?'

'Er – now, let me see,' I reply. 'I'll just get my diary.' It doesn't do for anyone to be too sure of you. Then I say, 'Well, I'm not sure, there's a possible in here for tomorrow night.'

'Well, cross it out and put in a dead cert. Me and

James, my flatmate, are coming down to see you tomorrow night, just before *Who Do You Woo?* starts. Then we're going to take you out clubbing. Okay?' Without waiting for an answer, he goes on, 'Jade, I've got something well crucial to ask you tomorrow.'

'What?'

'Oh, I can't ask you over the phone.'

'Why?'

He becomes the shy schoolboy. 'Cos it's too personal.'

'Oh, come on, tell me.'

'I can't, not on the phone. It's far too private.'

'Rupert, tell me.'

'All right, it's,' and then the pips start to go. 'Sorry,' he laughs. 'No more money. You'll just have to . . .'

And then we're cut off, leaving me about to explode with curiosity.

Friday, 19 February:
'How Would You Like to Be Famous for a Lot Longer?'

At four o'clock I'm interviewed on Cary Steven's radio show. Afterwards he says, 'Amazing, you didn't dry up once. If only all my guests were like you.' Then he asks me if I'll go on the local hospital radio. He began his broadcasting career there (when he was still at school) and still revisits it regularly.

'A lot of the patients really enjoy *Who Do You Woo?*' he says. 'So I know it would give them such a lift to hear an interview with someone from the programme.' He smiles. 'I mean, sod radio, it's people from the telly who are the real stars now.'

'Well, in that case, of course I'll go on. No problems, Cary.'

I just can't believe how prized I've suddenly become.

But then, that's what going on TV does for you; it gives you a mystical new power. That's why my very presence can give a lift to people I've never met. I've been given a wonderful gift and I promise to use it wisely. I mean, I'll never ever turn down anything for charity. Even if it's the other side of the country. If they want me, I'll be there.

I stop the taxi at the shopping precinct just before my house. I've a few minutes before *Who Do You Woo?* starts so I think I'll go for a quick stroll as there's a few people about and their reaction to me still knocks me out. I cross over to the newsagent – it's one of the few shops still open – and I'm about to go in when I freeze. For coming out of the shop is Adam. And he sees me but then deliberately looks away and I do the same.

So, now we're invisible to each other: a year has vanished in less than a week. I watch him trudge past me, head down, an old man's walk. And seeing him like that gives me this awful choked-up feeling – you know, when you can't even swallow properly. But then I think, he ruined my first television appearance and now he's ruining my second. Only, I won't let him this time. And I run home, determined to wipe Adam from my mind. In the driveway is an unfamiliar car. Rupert must be here already. He is. I see him in the lounge, reading the congratulations card my dad sent me.

'And here she is . . . the girl I picked,' he cries. Then he points to the guy on the settee. 'That ugly git, by the way, is James.'

James isn't exactly ugly but he looks a lot younger than eighteen, largely, I think, because he's got bright red cheeks and doesn't look as if he's started to shave yet.

'Hi, how are you hanging?' he says.

'You can't ask girls that,' says Rupert and they both snigger.

Mum joins us in the lounge when *Who Do You Woo?* starts. She's quite friendly but I sense a growing impatience and irritation with all this. I think she wants it to be over now. She certainly doesn't understand what this means to me, any more than Adam did.

But having Rupert there with me more than makes up for everything else. We keep looking at each other and then at ourselves on the screen, not quite believing we belong to those images up there. Then at the end I'm shown standing with Rupert and the camera keeps getting closer and closer until it isn't just photographing my face, but going right inside me. You can actually see my feeling of joy, actually see it swelling inside me. And it's as if I'd bared my private soul without my even realising. It was quite a shock, really.

Immediately the programme finishes the phone starts jangling and when I tell callers that Rupert is with me now they get so excited. He says 'Hello' to both Kay and Liz as well as Dad.

I keep asking Rupert what he wanted to ask me on the phone last night. But all he will say is, 'Can't ask you here. Not private enough.'

Then, just as he promised, Rupert takes me night-clubbing, with James as chauffeur. We join this queue of brightly coloured posers outside this club in Covent Garden. ('Absolutely the place to be seen,' apparently.) James goes ahead to see if he can get us in more quickly – he knows one of the bouncers – and then Rupert asks, 'How would you like to be famous for a lot longer?'

'Yes, sure,' I say.

He shifts about on his feet for a moment. 'This is mighty embarrassing,' he says.

'What is? Come on, tell me.'

'Okay, here goes. I know someone in Fleet Street who'll take our pictures tomorrow morning.'

'Great.'

'He'll also bring a reporter along. But there is one catch.'

'I've got to dance again.'

He smiles briefly. 'No, much worse. You've got to get engaged to the sexiest guy in the world.'

I give him what you might call a long, meaningful look. He immediately turns away.

'Why have we got to get engaged?' I ask his back.

He whirls round, the words rushing out. 'Because it's a much better story – you know – couple find true love on *Who Do You Woo?* All that crap. No – it's not crap. It's true.'

'Is it true?'

'Sure. You're my fantasy girl, you know that. Stop fishing for compliments.'

'So, we are getting engaged – really.' I don't know how else to explain what I mean.

'Really and truly,' says Rupert. 'And don't say this is so sudden, because you've had at least two minutes to get used to the idea.' Then his light tone slips away and he says, 'This is our chance, Jade. We could be in every paper across the country. We could be household names. And when you get a chance like this you've got to seize it, make the most of it. So, say yes.'

The words he's using go straight to my heart. Only Rupert understands what fame means to me. He's almost like my soul mate.

He makes as if to go down on one knee. 'Marry me, Jade, and you will never have to return to a life of drab obscurity again,' he says. 'I promise.' Now he is down on one knee and people are turning round and watching.

'Get up, Rupert,' I whisper, half amused, half embarrassed.

'Not till you say yes.'

I laugh. 'Oh yes, yes, yes.' How can I refuse my soul mate?

Rupert shoots up and hugs me and tells James who also hugs me. Then James tells the bodyguard who doesn't hug me but gives us a friendly wave as we jump ahead of the queue.

Once inside Rupert sets his watch to time how long it'll be before someone recognises us. To his horror, nearly an hour goes by before anyone realises we're 'someone'. Then this girl staggers over to us – she is very drunk – and recognises Rupert as 'off the telly'. Next she turns to me. 'You're the one who fell over. How are you?' She greets us like friends from her school, then rushes off to spread the word. Soon a steady trickle of people are plying us with questions and kisses. (Everyone wants to kiss us for some reason.) Rupert is grinning all over his face now and puts his arm around me, saying, 'Just wait till we're in the papers as well. We're going to need our own bodyguards soon.'

It's after two o'clock before I'm back home. Rupert insists on jumping out of the car and seeing me to the door.

'I am a gentleman,' he declares before skidding on to our grass. He'd forgotten how icy the paths were. He isn't hurt though and he just lies there, shaking with laughter, before pulling me down beside him. Then James gets out of the car and he's laughing too. His laugh would wake the dead – and does. Lights are popping on all down our road.

'Isn't that pretty?' says Rupert. 'All the lights are coming on. One day we'll be asked to switch on the lights at Christmas.'

'They're our neighbours' lights, actually,' I hiss, 'and they're all probably furious.'

But Rupert just calls out, 'Hello, neighbours, come out and join the party.' Then he starts kissing my thighs.

I finally bundle him into the car. He holds my hand, kisses me on the forehead, then tumbles across the back seat.

'Look after him,' I say to James. 'I'm getting engaged to him in nine hours' time.'

'Don't worry about him,' replies James. 'I've seen him much worse than this.'

Saturday, 20 February:
I Impersonate a Diving Board

Rupert's waiting for me at Leicester Square tube station at eleven o'clock, just as we'd planned. And he looks remarkably good, considering the state he was in last night. And he's rarin' to go. 'I'm on atomic fuel now,' he says.

Yesterday I was on atomic fuel, too, but this morning I feel bleary and rather strange, actually.

Just before we go into the studio, Rupert says, 'Hang about, I nearly forgot. Give me your left hand, third finger, the finger nearest to your heart, they say. Hey, what's this imposter doing here?' He's pointing at the ring with the two hearts. The one Adam gave me on our anniversary. Somehow I'd never gotten round to taking it off.

'It's just a ring I like,' I say.

'Cheap and nasty. Off with it,' he says.

I take the ring off and start putting it on another finger.

'Jade,' he says, mock sternly. 'What are you doing? You're only wearing one ring today.'

So I put Adam's ring into my handbag while Rupert slips on my finger a rather magnificent engagement ring – made of sapphires and diamonds.

'I've borrowed the ring from a good friend,' says Rupert. 'And she told me we can keep it as long as we like.'

I try and take in the ring's alien glitter while a picture runs through my mind, a picture of Geoff giving Clare her engagement ring at that New Year's Eve party. And then Clare coming over to me and whispering, 'It's your turn next – yours and Adam's.'

I'm introduced to the photographer – a small, untidy-looking man with a thick beard, who murmurs encouraging things as he snaps our picture. And Rupert has to keep placing the ring on my finger, again and again. In the end it's as if a piece of time has got stuck, as one moment is repeated over and over.

Perhaps that's why my mind won't stay still and keeps running away from the moment. For this moment doesn't seem quite real, somehow. In fact, I feel as if I am watching an image of myself again, just like I did on television last night. And then the reporter arrives and asks questions for hours and hours.

'When do you both intend to get married?' he asks.

Rupert grins – that magic grin of his. 'Oh, give us a chance. We've got things to do first.'

'Like what?' asks the reporter.

'Like shoot around the galaxy for a while,' says Rupert. He smiles again and so do I. Even though I haven't a clue what he's talking about. But he goes on talking. None of it seems to make any sense. Not that it matters. For what's happening now seems tiny and far away.

It's after two o'clock when we leave. James goes back to the flat. Rupert and I walk around London for a while. And this helps me feel more myself again. For the streets are packed and over and over we're greeted – and so warmly, too. Rupert keeps holding up my hand with the engagement ring on, calling out, 'Watch the papers tomorrow.'

Then Rupert takes me back to his flat and it's nothing like I'd imagined – but then, very few things are. I mean, it's not grand at all, just three poky, grubby rooms – bedroom, bathroom, kitchen, while all Rupert's entertaining takes place downstairs in the garage. There you will find a washing machine, a settee, two television sets, a pair of skis and a dry, musty smell you associate with old junk shops. And that is exactly what this garage resembles: a junk shop where nothing ever gets sold.

James brings back a curry – and I've never realised just how depressing that smell is. Then we lie, sprawled across

183

the carpet, while James and Rupert become more and more drunk.

Rupert is so different now – so many blokes are when their mates are around. And as I watch Rupert sniggering and fooling about with James, I realise I've become engaged to someone I hardly know, and, right now, I don't particularly like. I lie there wishing I hadn't rung Mum to tell her I'm staying the night with Rupert's family. For I want to be in my own bedroom with James Dean and Marilyn Monroe looking down on me, not stuck in this stranger's slum any more.

Suddenly, Rupert and James disappear. I look at my watch, it's nearly eleven. I hope the evening's over and I can just crash out somewhere now. But then Rupert returns looking really worried.

'What's wrong?' I ask.

'Oh nothing, nothing,' says Rupert so absently, so off-handedly, I flinch. He's talking to me now as if I am a casual acquaintance. I'm his fiancée, aren't I?

Suddenly James reappears – a look of triumph on his underdeveloped face. 'They were under your bed all the time,' he says. He could have been throwing a packet of cigarettes at Rupert – but they aren't cigarettes.

After much winking and giggling James disappears and Rupert pads over to me. He fingers the packet of condoms James has given him, then his eyes go up to his eyebrows as if he's reading an autocue. 'I always believe in practising safe sex,' he pronounces.

Yes, he is reading off an autocue. His own private one. Here's what you say to your Saturday-night lay. And that's all he sees. I'm just his latest blow-up doll.

I lie back on the carpet. Despite all my plans, all my dreams, I'm here lying in a dirty room full of cigarette smoke with someone who's forgotten I exist. But then, this is how everything ends up, isn't it? No matter how hard you struggle, in the end you're defeated, aren't you? Because that's what life, real life is: dark and shabby and cruelly disappointing.

My head aches. I feel tired and I want to be alone. I sigh and close my eyes like a patient waiting to go under the anaesthetic before a painful operation. And I see Adam, walking away from me. Adam – please understand. I need to be loved. That's all. Can't you understand? But he just walks on, further and further away from me. Until I can't see him any more.

And then Rupert is on top of me. Was it only last night I thought he was my soul mate? How can I have deluded myself so foolishly? Very easily. Right now I despise myself. But I despise Rupert even more. I want to tell him to get off, to leave me alone. But something stops me. His face. Maybe it's the dim, yellow light that makes Rupert's face look so pale and waxy and eerie. And he's not smiling like he was all the time on television, and without that smile his face has a vacant, unoccupied look.

If I tell him to get off me will he turn nasty, get angry? I don't know. I just know I suddenly feel very vulnerable. No, I won't say anything. I'll just lie here and let him call me 'tight' or 'frigid' or any of those words he probably uses.

I close my eyes.

'You can move around a bit, you know,' he says.

But I don't move. Can't. I just lie there like a diving board, until Rupert springs up. 'What is it with you? You've been coming on to me all week and now – don't you want it now?'

I sit up as well. I was getting very squashed down there. 'No, thank you,' I say. I could have been refusing a second cup of coffee.

'Why?' He's amazed, disbelieving. 'Don't you fancy me any more?'

I look at him. Only a kind of stale glitter clings to him now.

'I don't find the surroundings very romantic,' I say.

He stares hard at me as if trying to get me into focus. 'What's wrong with them?' he demands.

'They're dingy and squalid and – raw,' I say. He gives me another piercing look as if he is really searching in his memory for something. And then he says, 'So you want romance, do you?'

'Yes, I do. Sorry.'

He smiles, but the smile quickly melts away. Then he bows slightly. 'I apologise for not giving you romance and for all my other shortcomings.' He's mocking me. But I don't care. Anything is better than that glazed, vacant stare he's been giving me.

Then all at once he's the contrite schoolboy again. 'You're not cross with me, are you, Jade?' It's the first time he's used my name in hours.

'I drink too much,' he says, 'as I find *talking* to girls very difficult.' And with that he runs off.

He comes back laden with sheets and blankets. His mocking tone returns too. 'Don't worry, Jade,' he says. 'You will be quite undisturbed for the rest of the night.'

I know he feels hurt and degraded now. Well, so do I.

Despite his promise, I keep the yellow light on all night and I lie awake for ages. And then I dream. I'm walking by a stream, the one I saw with Adam after our anniversary meal. Only now the stream is iced over and there's not even one star out this time. Even the grass has been frozen into tiny white blades. There is nothing here any more but a terrifying stillness.

I am woken by the telephone. I shoot up. A few stray beams of light are easing their way through the cracks. I look at my watch. It's after eight. Then I hear voices on the stairs, Rupert's and James's voices. They seem angry.

But they are too muffled for me to make out what they are saying. I expect them to open the garage door but they don't. Then there's silence, strange and empty, just like in my dream. Nearly half an hour passes before I hear their voices again. They are louder now, especially Rupert's. He sounds really worked up. I put my ear to the door but I still can't pick up what they are talking about. I shudder. Has something bad happened?

I'm not sure whether to go upstairs or not. I want to but I'm also scared. A couple of times I walk right up to the door but then I lose my nerve. Finally though, the door opens and James stands there.

And for one crazy moment I expect him to drop some food down and then go away, locking the door behind him – just as if I were their prisoner. But of course he doesn't. Instead he gives his usual smile and asks, 'Fancy some breakfast?' – all bright and breezy.

'Yeah, sure.' I trudge up the stairs after him. 'Where's Rupert?' I ask.

His voice lowers. 'He's in the kitchen. He's pretty cut up, actually. It's best if he tells you about it.'

A feeling of dread twists my stomach as we squash into the kitchen. Rupert is hunched over the table which is covered in newspapers. My first thought is, There's something bad about us in the papers. Have they found out I have a steady boyfriend? But then Rupert waves one of the papers in front of me and I see not my face but someone else's. Someone who looks horribly familiar.

'She's beaten us,' says Rupert.

I pick up the paper. There is Magenta with her arm round Clive, the guy who Laura had picked on *Who Do You Woo?* The headline reads, Who Do You Marry? and underneath it begins, 'Last week, hunky Clive was picked up by Laura as her date on *Who Do You Woo?* But at the party afterwards Laura was forgotten, for it was love at first sight when Clive met Magenta. She had sung 'I'm Just a Girl Who Can't Say No' in the second half of the show and lost. But she certainly stole Clive's heart.

'Two-timing Clive was seen by millions kissing Laura on their date on Friday's *Who Do You Woo?* But yesterday Clive married his true love, Magenta, at a registry office ceremony in London. Said Clive, "I told Laura and she's thrilled for us. Like everyone, she thinks Magenta's a great girl."

'Laura Jacobs was unavailable for comment last night. But Magenta, who's hoping to become a full-time singer, says, "I've always been a girl who can say no, until I met Clive. As soon as we met I knew I couldn't live without him." Read full exclusive story of TV's real-life love affair on page seven.'

The story could also be read exclusively in four other papers, one of which even had an agony aunt analysing love at first sight and Magenta and Clive's chances of happiness. Another paper had pictures of Magenta and Clive splashed across two pages with the headlines ' "I can't fight love" says *Who Do You Woo?* star Magenta.' STAR! She's not a star. She didn't even win. I did. So surely I'm more of a star than her?

'Trevor says this kills our engagement story stone dead,' cries Rupert, then he slumps back in his chair.

James takes over explaining. 'Trevor is Rupert's mate in Fleet Street, the one who organised your pictures. He was the one who broke the news to us. He said once this Magenta story broke no one wanted to know about your engagement story.' He hands me a cup of tea, says, 'I'll leave you to talk it over,' and retreats upstairs, while Rupert and I stare gloomily at each other.

'We should have got married,' says Rupert. 'You've got to think big and we didn't think big enough. I suppose it's too late for us to get married now?'

'Yes,' I say firmly. 'It is.'

Rupert stares at me for a moment, his eyes seeming colourless today, then sinks back in his chair again. Funny, when they're dejected, both he and Adam look quite similar. They both seem totally weighed down by the problem. Only, there's a look in Rupert's eyes – a haunted look – I've never seen in Adam's face.

Strangely enough, I actually feel more sorry for Rupert

than I do for myself. And I really want to say something reassuring to cheer him up. I could always cheer Adam up. But Rupert, I don't know what to say to him because I hardly know him, really. All we had in common was a dream. We shared a dream. And now that's taken away from us, well, there's nothing else.

In the end I say, 'Rupert, one of us could still get discovered. A TV producer might have been watching.'

'That's true,' he replies but I know his mind is elsewhere.

James drives me back to the tube station while Rupert sits in the back looking dazed and bewildered. I don't feel half so bad as him about it. But then, the dream had already ended for me.

As I get out of the car Rupert comes to life again. He kisses me on the forehead, says, 'This is still our time,' and to my surprise hugs me hard. 'We nearly did it, didn't we?' he says and there are tears forming in his eyes now.

'Ring me some time,' I say.

'I might just do that.'

But I know he won't. For him, I've already faded into long shot. And before he's back in the car I'll be out of view.

So, goodbye, Rupert. For a whole week I thought I was in love with you. I looked into your eyes and saw – my reflection. It was that which I fell in love with, of course.

Now Rupert's out of my life forever. But suddenly I hear footsteps running behind me. And I hear someone calling my name, loudly, urgently. 'Jade, Jade.' I swing round. It's James and he's so out of breath he can't speak for a moment.

'Jade – I've a message for you – from Rupert,' he gasps.

'Yes?' I lean forward.

'He says can he have his ring back, please?'

Friday, 5 March:
Where Are They Now?

The snow's slipping away. Now nothing's left but a dirty brown sludge.

Everything's slipping away. The last couple of days I've been feeling a bit low, to tell the truth. So, to cheer myself up, I go into Hitchin. Yet, despite walking around for over an hour, I'm not stopped once.

But then I go into McDonalds and I see the boy behind the counter staring hard at me. After he's taken my order he comes back and says, 'It was you, wasn't it . . . ? You were on *Who Do You Woo?*' I say, 'Yes', and immediately put him at his ease. Soon we are laughing together and he tells me how glad he is that I won and adds, 'I've still got you on my video.' He gives me an extra portion of chips, too.

Well, that really cheers me up. I certainly think I am very good at meeting my public now, which makes it even more of a shame that my public is disappearing so quickly. Last week, so many other people stopped me. Where are they now?

I arrive home to find a letter from – do you remember the boy who sent me a photograph of a gerbil (how could you forget)? Well, this time he's sent me a picture of a parrot. He's cut the picture out and stuck it on a card, and then coloured it all in. I am very touched. And he signs his letter, 'Lovingly yours.'

So. Someone still loves me.

Monday, 15 March:
Jade Becomes a Missing Person

It's over.

This morning I walk into the greengrocer's and Mrs Almond says, 'Hello Jennifer. Mum all right?'

I just gape at her in horror and disbelief. A few weeks ago she'd called me Jade, and hung on my every word. But now she sees only dull, dreary Jennifer again. And today no one smiles or comes up to tell me about their life. They've forgotten all about Jade. And so quickly, too.

I walk out not knowing or caring where I'm going and tears are falling down my face now. But it's not me crying. It's Jade. She doesn't want to be invisible again.

Monday, 29 March:
Letter from Carly Carter

I wrote to Carly Carter to ask him what I should do next. I got his reply today. It was quite a friendly letter, but basically it just said I should get as many exams as possible, remember that most actors are unemployed . . . all the usual.

When I looked at the letter more closely I noticed my name was in a slightly darker type to the rest of the letter. He must have a standard letter he sends out. And that's all I've received. So I'm back to writing to computers.

I'm really trying not to give up. It's just when I think of my future – well, those shades have snapped down tightly again. And I can't see anything.

Thursday, 15 April:
News of Adam

I sit staring into my mirror. Today there is nothing there but darkness. Then, out of the darkness comes a voice, male and hearty.

INTERVIEWER: And my next guest on *I've Got a Problem* is Jade. Good evening, Jade.

ME: Please go away.

INTERVIEWER (*ignoring this*): Jade, you're through to *I've Got a Problem*, so share your problem with us. And don't worry, we can't see your unwashed hair and red eyes. The screen is all blacked out.

ME: Go away.

INTERVIEWER (*laughing nervously*): Perhaps if I prompt you a little, then. I understand you had a nasty shock this afternoon. Am I right? (*I do not answer.*) I believe you switched on the television this afternoon and you saw Magenta singing!

ME (*suddenly*): Singing! She wasn't singing. Nothing musical could come out of that tight little mouth.

INTERVIEWER: Now, you mustn't become bitter.

ME: Why not? She stole my chance. It should have been me up there this afternoon. I won the competition. Not her.

INTERVIEWER: I think we'd better change the subject. Now, we hear you haven't been out of the house for days, weeks even. Is this right?

ME (*dully*): Yes, that's right.

INTERVIEWER: When exactly was the last time you went out, Jade?

ME: I don't remember. Yes, I do. It was a week ago last Tuesday. I'd gone up to London just to see if anyone would stop me. I still couldn't believe it was all over, you see. But it was – and no one came up to me, oh, except for this old woman in a dirty brown coat. She looked at me and I smiled. And then she started shouting at me, 'You think you're the little duchess, don't you? Well, you're not.'

INTERVIEWER: What did she mean by that?

ME: Haven't a clue. She said some other things, too. None of which made any sense. And I wanted to help, so I tried replying to her. But nothing I said seemed to get through to her. In fact, if anything she just became angrier. In the end she just went off and started shouting at someone else. And I thought, she's gone so far into her own world now, that no one can reach her any more. She's totally alone.

INTERVIEWER: Like you.

ME: No, of course not like me.

INTERVIEWER: But aren't you more alone now than you've ever been before?

ME: Stop this interview.

INTERVIEWER: Ah, so we've hit on the truth. Not even Adam has bothered to contact you, has he? Every day you've been hoping he will. Especially as you're wondering if the break-up was all your fault. Didn't Ryan tell you that you had a ruthless streak? Well, when stardom beckoned you were pretty ruthless with Adam. You . . .

ME: No, no, stop.

INTERVIEWER: All in all, Jade, I'd say you're an ideal candidate for *I've Got a Problem*. In fact, we could probably do a whole series on you.

ME: Look, just leave me alone. Go!

I close my eyes. There's silence for a moment then I hear my name being called over and over. Only now I'm being called Jenny; even in my dreams I end up as Jenny. But then I hear Jenny called again, only much louder this time. I whirl round from my mirror. My mum's standing right behind me.

'I've been calling and calling you,' she says.

'Oh, sorry, I didn't hear you.'

'There was a phone call for you from Liz. She said she had some news about Adam.'

Just hearing his name now seems to cut somewhere deep inside me. But I must remain calm, uninvolved. 'What news is that?'

'Liz didn't say. She wants you to ring her back. And she's going out in a few minutes, so you'd better ring her back now.'

'Okay,' I say, then lie back on my bed.

My mum watches me with some exasperation. She thinks I should be charging downstairs now. But why should I, just to hear that Adam's got a new girlfriend or something? Everyone, even your best friend, loves telling you things like that. And I'm supposed to say, 'That's great. I'm really happy for him.' And I would be if only – if only Adam wasn't still hanging about my memory banks like a bad smell. He's forgotten me but I can't forget him. Ah well, Mum'd say it's what I deserve. She's still hovering over me.

'I'll ring Liz later, Mum. I'm too tired now.' I close my eyes. 'Bye then.'

But Mum doesn't take my unsubtle hint. Instead she says ominously, 'We must TALK.'

'Oh no, not now, Mum, please.'

'Yes, now,' says Mum. 'And sit up properly. You're not ill, are you?'

I reluctantly sit up. And the way Mum's looking at me – it's like having a searchlight shone in your face. 'Your mother doesn't miss a thing,' the editor from her paper once said. And I half-expect her to get a notebook out now. Perhaps she can write up our conversation afterwards for one of her child psychology classes.

'Now look, Jen, we can't have you hiding up here like this, can we . . . ? So come on, love, tell me what's wrong. Only, don't tell me you want to be famous, please! I have had it up to here with that nonsense.' She laughs half-heartedly.

'It's not nonsense,' I mutter, glaring at her.

'Yes, it is. You can't build your life on dreams.'

'But dreams can become reality. Still, you'll never understand what I mean, so there's absolutely no point in us having this conversation.'

I wrap my arms about myself while Mum stands in front of my mirror, looming over me like an interrogator. She doesn't reply for a moment, just goes all tight-lipped. But then she says wearily, 'All right, Jenny, tell me why you want to be famous.'

'No, there's no point, you . . .'

'Look, I want to understand. So come on, explain it to me.'

I lean forward. It would be wonderful if she could understand. 'All right. When I appeared on television my whole life changed. I can't explain it, except by saying it was as if I had this marvellous new power. You remember that story you read me once, about this guy who finds everything he touches turns to gold? Well, it was a bit like that. Only, it wasn't objects that turned to gold, it was my life. All the drab, boring bits of my life were suddenly transformed. And all the pieces seemed to fit together. And, Mum, the feeling it gives you. You feel so high, really high . . .'

'A cheap drug,' interrupts Mum. 'That's all your fifteen seconds' fame was. As soon as your fame runs out – well, look at you, lying up here like you're dying because you can't get your next fix!'

I'm so furious with her for saying that, I burst out, 'Cheap drugs! Well, you should know all about those – smoking yourself to death.'

It's my mum's turn to look startled. 'All right. You've got me there,' she concedes. 'But listen well to what I'm going to say, Jenny, because I'm right. Being famous isn't the answer to anything and it will never make you happy, not really happy.'

I turn away.

'No, don't look away from me. At least grant me the courtesy of listening to what I have to say.'

'Like you granted me.'

'Jenny, love, will you just listen for pity's sake! Don't you see what you're doing? You're handing over control of your life to other people. If they like you then you're happy. But if they don't or if they ignore you, then you're miserable again. Well, what kind of a way is that to live? Go on, answer me.'

'Mum, you think being famous is just being noticed and showing off – but it's not. It's about getting up before an audience and giving them something. For a few minutes you can take an audience out of themselves, give them pleasure. That's what I did on *Who Do You Woo?* And it's then I felt really in touch with myself. The real me . . .' I stop. My mum is staring blankly at me. I know she can't wait for me to finish so she can insert her next piece of advice. 'But you're not listening to me. You never listen. All you want to do is sit smoking cigarettes, playing the wise woman of the town, giving advice.'

'Now that's not fair.'

'It's true, though. Every time I speak to you now, it's lecture time.'

'Well, if I see you doing something stupid, what else can I do?'

'You could –' I stop. What exactly do I want Mum to do? I know what I mean but I can't find the right word. 'You could,' I repeat, 'show me a bit of sympathy.'

Sympathy isn't exactly what I mean and my mum swoops on the word. 'Sympathy!' She looks as if she's about to throw up. 'What the hell use is sympathy? I tell you, sympathy can be very cruel – don't I know. When your father left this house there were plenty of people ready to offer me sympathy and, thanks to their sympathy, I nearly went under.'

'You did?' I'm incredulous.

Mum sits down. 'When your father first left, everyone said I was so brave. But I wasn't brave, more like quietly confident. I was convinced he'd come back to me, you see.' She half smiles. 'How could he manage without me? I organised every part of his life. So I sat and waited for his humble return and waited.' She straightens my covers as she goes on. 'Then, when I realised he wasn't coming back and was coping very nicely without me – God, that hurt! Still does. And like I said, for a while there I felt as if I was under water and heading straight for the bottom.'

'What stopped you . . .?'

'Hitting the bottom? Friends. Proper friends. They pulled me up by making me face things as they are, by pushing me out, but most of all by helping me see that what's most important is you must feed what's in there.'

She taps her head. 'So then when you're dropped, and we all get dropped some time and when we least expect it too, then you won't break.'

Before I can reply the telephone starts ringing again. 'That'll be Liz,' I say softly.

'Shall I take it?' says Mum. 'I can tell her.'

'No, I'll answer it.' I stand up. 'I may as well know how Adam met this dishy blonde and is really happy we've finished.'

Mum squeezes my hand. 'Whatever the news is, you can face it.' Then she calls after me, 'And without any bloody sympathy from anyone, either.'

But when I pick up the phone it's not Liz's voice I hear, but Dad's. He's ringing to tell me Yvonne had a baby boy, seven pounds, two ounces. They're calling him Peter. And Dad's so chuffed. I'm sure he reckons if he can produce children then he must still be in his prime. Then he asks me, 'So, how do you feel about having a new half-brother?

'I haven't got a new half-brother. I've got a new brother,' I reply.

My dad develops a definite sob in his voice after I say that. And when I say I want to see Peter, well, I make his evening. I figure, with parents like that, poor Peter's going to need all the help he can get.

After Dad rings off, the phone goes again, almost immediately. I pick it up and this time I hear Liz's voice.

Friday, 16 April:
You Don't Want to Finish With Adam

I never thought I'd be returning to Adrianne's and Phyllis's Drama Club. Not after my last disastrous visit. And certainly not to see Adam in a play there. But this is the news Liz had for me. Then she suggests that we get together for a girls' night and go and see Adam's play, just for a laugh. Kay joins us, too. So for the first time this year, just the three of us go out together.

And we sit in the village hall on hard, uncomfortable seats, surrounded on all sides by family and friends of the cast. Adam's dad is there. I pretend not to see him. So is one of Adam's mates from work. I pretend not to see him either. I don't know why I'm here really. I mean, Adam and I finished months ago now.

Curiosity. Yes, that's it. I can't imagine Adam acting

in a play, so I've come to see what he's like. Actually, Adam isn't in this one very much. He plays one of the evacuees sent to the countryside during World War II. So he spends most of the play standing around in long shorts talking about how much he misses his local fish and chip shop. But he is good, better by far than all the others. I'll give him that. He even puts on quite a good accent. Actually, he's quite convincing – a rubbishy play, though.

Afterwards we have a drink in the pub right next to the theatre. I say, 'Won't the actors come in here? I don't want to see Adam.'

And Liz replies. 'Oh no, they all go to a quite different pub.'

A minute later the entire cast troop in. Some still have their make-up on and you can tell they think themselves real ACTORS now. Adam is there with someone I recognise from the drama club – Faber. She has her arm around him and immediately I feel myself tense up.

I say, 'I don't need this. Let's go, shall we?'

But Liz says she won't leave until she's finished her drink. And Kay says she really likes it there. Then suddenly Liz stands up.

'Where are you going?' I ask.

'Won't be long,' says Liz and I see her exchange a look with Kay before leaving.

'It's really nice the three of us out like this, isn't it?' says Kay desperately. 'Out on the town again ...' Her voice trails away.

I'm not answering her. I'm watching Liz walk straight over to Adam. Liz can be quite commanding when she wants and even Faber shrinks back.

'What is she talking to Adam about?'

'I don't know.'

'Yes, you do. And you've no right to interfere.' I should walk out. But it's Adam who walks out.

'Now look what's happened,' I hiss at Kay. 'I feel so degraded.' Kay hunches her shoulders together and tries to look invisible.

But then Liz comes back and says, 'I've got a message for you from Adam. He's got something to say to you and he'd like to talk to you outside.'

'I really don't care to talk to Adam,' I begin.

'Look, will you just listen to me?' cries Liz so loudly a few people turn round. 'Oh, I'm sorry for shouting but you're really annoying me tonight.'

'Me?'

'Yes, you, because you know full well you don't want to finish with Adam.'

'Excuse me – but I have finished with him. And anyway, when I first told you we'd finished you said you were pleased, as I could do much better for myself.'

'I know. That's why I encouraged Mark to introduce you to all those guys from the bank.'

'And a finer collection of chins I've never seen.'

'They weren't so bad,' says Liz. 'If I'd been you I'd have considered one or two at least.'

'Who?'

'Oh well, I'm not going into that now. Anyway, I'm nearly an old married lady. But, Jade, if you want Adam back, which you do –'

'Do I?'

'Yes, well, just don't expect him to be waiting around for ever, that's all. Because if I'm not mistaken, that girl over there, the one whose eyelashes don't quite reach her mouth . . .'

'Faber.'

'Whoever. Well, I wouldn't be surprised if she follows him out any second now. And once she does your chance could be gone and I don't know when there'll be another one.'

A cold chill runs through me. I stand up. 'All right. But I'm only going to please you two,' I say.

'You're so good to us,' says Liz. 'We'll see you tomorrow, then.'

'You'll probably see me in about two minutes,' I say.

Both Kay and Liz exchange smiles.

'And stop looking so pleased with yourselves,' I say. 'I'm only going to talk to him.'

Outside, Adam's leaning against this black car. As soon as he sees me he stands up straight. I don't say anything at first. It's hard to speak when your heart's beating like crazy.

'How are you?' he asks.

'I'm fine. You?' We are speaking as if we've both been away somewhere.

'Yeah, fine.'

'You were good tonight, by the way,' I say.

A smile creeps across his face. 'Oh, it was a very small part.'

'But you made it count.'

He smiles again. 'They were desperate for blokes, that's how I got the part.'

'And have you enjoyed it?' I ask, wondering how long we can remain on this safe topic.

'Well, I've been at a bit of a loose end recently and it's filled up some time, kept me busy. I expect you're very busy?'

'No, I'm not busy at all.'

'No more TV?'

'No,' I say.

He looks shocked. 'I can't understand that.'

'Neither can I.' I laugh nervously. 'Yet, it seems the one they want is Magenta – that's the girl who sang . . .'

'I remember. She was crap,' says Adam. Well, I suppose she'd be good for anyone with bowel trouble. A few bursts of her singing could certainly clear the old system up.'

I am smiling now. I'd forgotten how funny Adam can be. I lie. I haven't forgotten at all.

'When you were on television I thought you were very good,' he says suddenly.

'Oh, it's a long time ago now,' I say airily.

'No, you were. I mean, watching most of that show is like having your brain covered in slime. It's so artificial and forced. But you – you just jumped off the screen. You seemed so natural. Actually, after I saw you I thought, that's it, she's bound to get snapped up now.'

I start to laugh. 'I think me going on television was just one of destiny's many pranks. You know, let's get her hopes up, then . . .' I stop, realising how bitter I am sounding. I try and change gear. 'There are still one or two things I'm doing. Well, one, hospital radio.'

'If you'd been rubbish I could have handled it much easier,' says Adam suddenly.

'I should have told you about it – long before I did,' I reply, equally suddenly.

And, all at once, we're sighing with relief. We've

navigated our way through the tricky bit, the apologies. Now – just where do we go?

'Fancy a spin?' asks Adam, smiling proudly.

'A spin?'

'In my car.'

'Your car?'

'Passed my test two weeks ago last Wednesday. I don't know who was more amazed, me or my instructor. I'm still lousy at parking, though. As you can see, my car's only about a mile from the kerb.'

'But is this really your car?' I say.

'Well, the firm's. I started a new job as a salesman last Monday.'

'Selling what?'

He laughs nervously. 'Nothing brilliant. I sell biscuits. But it's more interesting than before; what wouldn't be? And you get to see a bit of the countryside.'

'Yeah, sounds great. I'm really pleased for you.'

'Well, in a way this is all thanks to you,' he says.

'To me?'

'When we finished I felt as if I'd had my insides kicked out. But then I got to thinking about myself and I wasn't very impressed. I should have pushed myself, gone for things a bit more.'

'Oh, no,' I begin.

'Oh, yes,' he grins, 'and don't interrupt. I've been

learning this speech for weeks. You've made me lose my thread now. Oh yeah, do you remember that film we saw about a young man in days long ago – he had a name like soap powder – who tries to win the hand of the beautiful maiden he loves, by going out and performing daring deeds?'

I nod.

'He goes into battle against the evil Medusa who can turn men into stone with just one glance. Well, I figured the modern equivalent of Medusa was Pilchards, so I went in and did battle with him. And in a way I won. I resigned. Now, this guy also went about slaying every monster who barred his way, like those giant forest scorpions you hated so much. Giant forest scorpions are practically extinct in Stevenage now but there are other monsters just as deadly lurking inside me and they've stopped me doing things for years. In fact, they very nearly stopped me taking my driving test and going for that salesman interview. But inspired by you and for you – I slayed them all. Or nearly all. There's still one left, the one who stopped me driving outside your house and laying all my deeds before you . . .'

'It's all right, the heroine slayed that one,' I say. 'In fact, all she asks of her hero is that he lets her go out and slay a few monsters for herself. As for those daring deeds, I'm impressed but not really surprised. I always thought you were pretty amazing. By the way, there's still the last scene to play.' I smile. 'The one where the hero sweeps the heroine into his arms.'

We do a first take of that. And a second. And a third . . .

Friday, 7 May:
My Dream

Adam rings. 'Hi, Jen,' he says. 'Oh shit, I'm sorry. I'm really sorry. I mean Jade.'

'It's all right,' I say at once. 'I answer to most things. It doesn't matter.'

Actually, it does. I hate being called any name other than Jade – but not so much that I want to give Adam grief about it. And we're so anxious not to upset each other now. It's almost funny. I guess we're making up for the careless way we treated each other before.

Then we talk about Brighton. Adam's managed to change his booking for the end of June.

'We'll definitely make Brighton this time, won't we?' he says. 'I mean, even if we get trapped under a cooling tower five seconds before we leave, we'll still scramble out and . . .'

Yes, Brighton is waiting for us on the horizon just like before. And Adam will be picking me up for the cinema in twenty minutes, just like before. Only this time he's driving to the Multiplex in Milton Keynes. And before he gets here I want to tell you something. Would you believe, I have two jobs now.

Firstly – and quickly – I'm back at Vaughan's – been back nearly three weeks. Yesterday Ryan banged the gong for me. And I enjoyed it but I didn't believe it this time, if you know what I mean. Selling is like stardom really, too slippery and unpredictable to put at the centre of your life. And yet, when Ryan banged that gong for me again, it was just like being given a huge shot of adrenalin. And I'm still hooked on that feeling. I must admit that.

As for my second job: if ever you find yourself in a hospital near Stevenage, switch on your radio on Sunday morning and you'll find – me.

Yes, really. For I've my own show on hospital radio and I have, oh, at least eleven listeners. No, it's going all right actually. Every Sunday I do two hours: requests, messages – you know the sort of thing, plus a few thoughts of my own. It takes quite a lot of preparation though.

Adam has to help me pick the music.

And last Sunday Gary Stevens (he's the one who interviewed me on the radio) came by, heard me and afterwards said I was nearly as good at talking rubbish as he was. He also said he'd put a word in for me at his radio station next time they're recruiting.

When I told Adam all this he was really enthusiastic, actually he was a bit too enthusiastic. I mean, I knew he was pretending to be more impressed than he really was. He still doesn't quite understand my dream. While my mum still thinks that wanting to be famous is just chasing fool's gold.

Perhaps it is. But it's my dream. My chance to touch the heights. *Mine*. And whatever happens I'll never let it escape. For if I do, then I will be lost too. *Who Do You Woo?* was only a first step, I know that. But it did prove that I have a few particles of talent – as well as giving me some stories to tell my grandchildren. And I plan to have a lot more stories to tell them.

Incidentally, I heard something mighty interesting on the radio yesterday. Did you know they are looking for couples to appear on a new TV show? And each week the whole show will be about just one couple. So Adam and I could be on screen for thirty whole minutes. All we have to do are a few compatibility tests (and Adam and I are very compatible) and then a psychiatrist says what our chances are of staying together (well, we know that, very good).

Anyway, I was so excited I even mentioned the show to Adam last night, but only in a very light-hearted way.

And Adam cracked up. He thought the whole idea was hilarious.

'Adam's here,' calls Mum suddenly.

'I'm there,' I cry, flinging on a coat.

I pick up Adam's scarf. He left it here last night. But then I put it back. It's a warm evening. He won't need it tonight. At the door Mum is waving to Adam (who's posing away in his car. He gets such a big kick out of being behind that wheel).

'And is that Kay in the back?' asks Mum.

'That's right. Stevie Lee's got a tiny role in this film, so Kay's mad to see it. She's been talking about nothing else for days.'

Mum shakes her head. 'It meets a need, I suppose, like the strange objects in those shops in Soho.'

The second I step outside Adam is out of his car and opening the door for me, grinning away.

And I think how good he's going to look on television with me.

We'll be a sensation, won't we?